Andrew Sloan Draper

The Rescue of Cuba

an episode in the growth of free government

Andrew Sloan Draper

The Rescue of Cuba
an episode in the growth of free government

ISBN/EAN: 9783337378431

Printed in Europe, USA, Canada, Australia, Japan

Cover: Foto ©Andreas Hilbeck / pixelio.de

More available books at **www.hansebooks.com**

The
Rescue of Cuba

*An Episode in the Growth
of Free Government*

By:
Andrew S. Draper, LL.D.
President of University of Illinois

Silver, Burdett and Company
Boston   New York   Chicago

MDCCCXCIX

TO THE HEROIC YOUTH

OF OUR COUNTRY

WHO AT THE CALL OF DUTY DO NOT HESITATE TO

OFFER THEIR LIVES FOR FREEDOM AND THE FLAG.

Preface

THIS book has been written for young Americans. Its purpose is twofold : it aims, first, to exhibit the war of 1898 as one more step, and an important step, in the steady progress of the world towards universal liberty ; it also aims to offer such a faithful picture of the heroism and manly quality of the American soldiers and sailors who gave their lives for the rescue of their oppressed neighbors, as may help my young countrymen to realize what it costs to extend free institutions, and to appreciate what it means to be an American citizen.

The story of the slow movement of the human race out from the dark ages of universal tyranny into the modern age of freedom, enlightenment, and equality has never yet been clearly taught in our schools below the universities. For the last six or seven centuries the world has been moving from densest ignorance towards the era of the common school for everybody ; from continuous disorder, warfare, and robbery, to peaceful commerce and safe industry ; from the unbridled power of kings and nobles, to the security of a free, law-abiding state ; from intolerance and persecution, to freedom of thought and liberty of speech.

In this steady progress the topics of our special histories are only episodes, and they can be fully understood only when the student is able to give them their proper setting as parts of the grand human movement towards liberty. This progress of the world towards emancipation has met terrible antagonism. Kings and nobles have been against it. Ignorance, intolerance, and selfishness have always been in opposition to it. It has occasioned the greatest battles of history and has brought out the most conspicuous heroes of the race. Every free land has been made free by the richest human blood shed for liberty.

The battles for freedom have done more than mark the people's advance towards liberty ; these struggles have also quickened their wits, strengthened their manhood, and thus further qualified them to hold and enjoy the civil liberty they have gained.

The expulsion of Spain from Cuba by the United States was only an episode in this world-wide contest for self-government. In the unselfish, neighborly, and resolute spirit which prompted it, in the magnificent heroisms which it revealed, and in the uplift which it gave to the good cause of popular liberty in all parts of the world, it was a remarkable part of the long, continuous, and not yet ended contest.

The quickness and completeness with which the thing was done has been a surprise to ourselves as well as to the watching world. The explanation of this my young readers will doubtless find, to their own satisfaction, in the strangely different characters of the two races that fought.

There was great bravery on both sides. The weapons and the fleets were, all things considered, not unequally matched; if our ships were better equipped, they were no more numerous or formidable, while the Spanish army was certainly better provided and larger in numbers than ours.

Our real superiority was in the traits and training of our people. On our side were hardy manhood, self-reliance, clear and accurate calculation, mechanical skill, and willingness to do any kind of work that necessity demanded. On the other side there was a great deal of bombast, conceit, and vanity; there was a signal absence of good forecast and of shrewd, exact planning; there was a sense of helpless dependence on somebody else; there was a lack of manual skillfulness; there was a love of ease at the wrong time, and a foolish pride that made certain kinds of labor seem unworthy.

A nation's ideal of sport is closely related to its physical strength and its fighting power. On the American side the notion of sport has been the baseball diamond and the football gridiron, with their tests of physical endurance, their dangers, their honest hurts, and their manly spirit; on the Spanish side it has been the bull-ring, with its frilled professionals, its butchery, and its depraved tastes.

The contest was that of highly trained and intelligent manliness on the one hand, against uneducated pertinacity and too much vainglory on the other; the methods of the modern expert matched against the belated habits of the mailed knights and men-at-arms of another age. The result of such a match was speedy and overwhelming.

Some of the later developments of the war and some of its results are not entirely relevant to the purpose of this book. Hence, while the movement towards "expansion" is not avoided, it has purposely been given a subordinate place. I have treated the war from the point of view of its true cause, not from the point of view of all its effects. Much of what has come afterward has been an afterthought.

The case is somewhat similar to that of our Civil War ; there, the wiping out of slavery was one enormous result, but the question whether the Union should be retained or dissolved was what roused the people to arms, and on that fact all judgments of that war must rest.

In our war with Spain it was not national expansion that caused the clash of arms. The action of the United States was forced by the people, and the people had not the remotest consciousness of a desire for more territory. They were disinterested. It is doubtful if they would have consented to the war, even on the destruction of the Maine, if there had not been, long before, a deep and right-hearted sympathy with their neighbors who, in fearful distress, were reaching for American freedom.

It was to rescue Cuba, not to gain Puerto Rico or the Philippines, that bound all sections and parties of our people together in a sublime demand for a resort to arms. The results are much greater than we thought, but they may be accepted in good conscience and with entire confidence.

In all this there is a wealth of inspiration for our American youth. A country that will fight, not for some commercial interest, but because, like the good Samaritan, it feels it has a duty to its suffering neighbor who has fallen among thieves, is a country worthy of our highest pride, our lasting faith, our utmost devotion. We may confidently follow the humane impulses of such a country to their logical conclusions, even though the road leads through fire and blood.

In the hope of making the most of these things for the good of our common citizenship, this little book is presented.

UNIVERSITY OF ILLINOIS, 1899.

Contents

CHAPTER VII

The Attack on Santiago (*Continued*)

CHAPTER VIII

Destruction of Cervera's Fleet

CHAPTER IX

The Winning of Cuba and Puerto Rico

CHAPTER X

The Fall of Manila and the Suit for Peace

CHAPTER XI

The Spirit of American Soldiers and Sailors

CHAPTER XII

The Results

List of Illustrations

THE RESCUE OF CUBA

CHAPTER I

Historic Misgovernment by Spain

IN the world's contest for freedom Spain has played a large part; but her part, as this chapter and the next will show, has been unhappily upon the wrong side. No other people ever had greater opportunities to attain first rank among the nations, and no other people was ever overwhelmed with greater humiliations or more dismal failure.

The Spanish people have many admirable characteristics. They are distinguished for their grave and careful courtesy to strangers and for their hospitality to visitors. They preserve a marked dignity of bearing; they are intensely patriotic; they are brave to the extremity of desperation. They have been in the past energetic and aggressive.

But along with these qualities are others which are the opposite of admirable. A proper pride is always to be respected, but Spanish pride is so excessive that, from an Anglo-Saxon point of view, it seems to turn easily into foolish vanity; it certainly leads the Spanish people frequently to deceive themselves rather than to admit that they have been wrong; and no people can make any progress unless they are willing to acknowledge their failings so that they can mend them. The chivalry and courtesy, which are so highly prized by the Spaniards, seem too often to be a thin crust of outward behavior, while below these pleasant manners may be selfishness and cruel feelings. Their dignified politeness is beautiful to experience, but underneath this sweetness of temper the world has discovered sad degrees of duplicity, intrigue, vindictiveness, and inhumanity. Moreover, the Spanish character has seemed to be almost hopelessly rapacious; the poor, ignorant peasants of course have to work, but most Spaniards of the more intelligent classes consider labor to be beneath them, and too many of them have been accustomed, even to the present, to follow the custom of the old dark ages and depend for their riches upon what they could wrench from those who were weaker than themselves, or else purloin from their own Government.

There are certainly many exceptions to this: there are good people in Spain, as everywhere; but corruption seems to prevail among Spaniards more widely and persistently than in any other European nation; it is the trait that has most undermined the Spanish character, and has been more effective than any other in retarding Spanish progress, while other European nations have grown more honest and humane with the progress of civilization. Corruption and cruelty have held backward a nation of splendid possibilities, and have led Spain to commit acts almost as unwise and atrocious as those of Turkey.

The situation of the Spanish peninsula is exceedingly important. Washed by the Atlantic on one side and the Mediterranean on another, commanding the gate of Gibraltar on the great highway of the nations, and separated from the body of Europe by a mountain range which is practically impassable against spirited defense, her territorial position has been one of strong and world-wide significance.

Outside of her home peninsula she has come into the possession of more territory and lost more territory than any other modern nation. Her arms and her diplomacy have, at one time or another, given her claim to dominion over those parts of Europe now held by Austria, Holland, Belgium, Alsace and Lorraine in Germany, Italy, and Portugal; while her discoveries and conquests gave her the greater and the richer part of North America, nearly all of South America, the West Indies, the Philippines, and other groups of rich islands in both hemispheres, as well as a large slice of Africa.

But her avarice, her illiberality, her intolerance of new opinions, her antagonism to liberty, her duplicity in dealing with other nations, her repeated attempts to repress manhood through cruelties, have caused nearly all these outside lands to be taken from her by more progressive powers, or else to leave her through their own revolutions.

Spain has not been without a civilization which was relatively high. She was the " Tarshish " of Scripture.

Her soil is rich in vegetable and mineral wealth. The time was when she had prosperous and famous cities, when the arts and sciences were cultivated, when she was at the front and gave promise of remaining at the front of the intellectual progress of the world. But her national policy of deceitfulness and cruelty arrested the intellectual and moral development of her people.

The discovery of America by Columbus, under Spain's auspices, gave her the chance to become a great empire. Her monarchs had just conquered the Moors, and had consolidated the various little Spanish kingdoms into one nation. Now the limitless quantities of gold which began to be sent to her in treasure-ships from America enabled her to enter a career of European conquest and successful enlargement which lasted for a good part of a century, until the dominions of Philip II. included, not only the entire Spanish peninsula, but Sicily and Sardinia, a large part of Italy, and a splendid kingdom around the Rhine, besides most of the Western Hemisphere and innumerable islands in the Pacific and Indian Oceans. He was said to be the monarch of one hundred million subjects.

No wonder Spain dreamed of extending her empire till it embraced the whole world. Her soldiers were the most numerous and daring, her fleets were the largest, her treasury was the richest, her opportunity was the best. Her dream of universal empire might possibly have been realized if her rule had been tinged with human sympathy or had paid respect to human rights.   But it was so cruel that even the ignorant and downtrodden peoples of those earlier days revolted.

She had an ingenious method for keeping her people in humble submission to her throne and for bringing other nations under the same subjection; it was the Spanish Inquisition, a system of torture and death for opinion's sake which was well calculated to strike terror to the strongest souls.

This was a scheme for secretly inquiring into the thoughts of the individual, and murdering him if his thoughts were not satisfactory to the crown.   Under the penalty of torture and death anyone might be required to inform against his neighbor, or even against members of his own household.   The inquisitors condemned without open trial.   A suspect was put upon the rack at midnight, in a dimly lighted dungeon, and his sinews stretched and his bones broken until life almost went out of the poor aching body, for the purpose of eliciting a confession of guilt or a charge against others.   This torture might be continued at frequent intervals, sometimes for years, only to let the wretched victim perish by burning at the stake at last.

The property of the condemned went to the king, and of course the possessors of wealth were early victims.   No man was safe.   Women and children were by no means exempt.   To refuse information or supposed information was to defy the merciless inquisitors, and to reveal any secret or alleged secret of the bloody tribunal was certain death.   The deceits which were used to entrap the unwary can scarcely be believed.

Death, in its most horrid form of lingering torture, claimed hundreds of thousands. The executions took place at stated times in the public squares and were attended by the officials of state and by the wretched people in vast crowds. Death was ordinarily by fire. Confession before the multitude purchased the poor privilege of being strangled by the garrote before the body was thrown into the flames.

Such a system must necessarily accomplish one of two ends, and that very completely. It must either drive a people to revolt, or it must utterly destroy their sense of manhood. In different parts of the empire it did both. The results turned upon the character of the people.

Thus, in the Spanish peninsula it stopped the wheels of progress. It drove out a million of Moors, Protestants, and Jews. The two former classes included the best mechanics and the cleverest artificers Spain ever had, and the Jews were her ablest bankers. To expel all these was to cut off the internal resources of national strength. The inquisitorial system also hurt those who remained in Spain by putting a premium on the arrogance of some and the subserviency of others, and thus robbed the people of much of their moral sense.

But when Spain undertook to put this system in operation among her subjects in the Netherlands, it there produced a revolution, the success of which gave a wonderful energy to the life of the liberty-loving Dutch, and, through them, opened the way for the advance of civilization throughout the world.

In 1568 the Spanish Inquisition condemned the three millions of people in the Netherlands to death because of their religious and political opinions, and a proclamation of the Spanish king at once confirmed the act. William the Silent led the Dutch revolt against the oppressor. It was the world's first great battle for the liberty of the individual. It continued for forty years. In it a hundred thousand Netherlanders laid down their lives for the rights of intellect and conscience. Words would fail to tell of the adventurous daring, of the intrigue and deceit, or of the atrocious cruelties of the Spanish. But the desperate heroism of the Dutch finally beat them back, gained recognition for their little Republic of seven states in 1609, and established the fullest liberty of thought and freedom of worship. They celebrated their victories by setting up schools and universities, and entered upon a career of intellectual and industrial progress. They had stood during most of the war utterly alone against the most powerful nation of Europe; their energy, industry, and virtue were so great that when their independence was gained they were as powerful as the English, and even more progressive; their ships were seen in every port; there was scarcely any beggary; and nearly every citizen could read and write.

Against this spirit in the Netherlands Spain proved powerless. We Americans are debtors to these Dutch patriots and defenders of freedom who delivered their country from the Spaniards; for it was from the Dutch Republic, quite as much as from England, that our forefathers got their ideas of liberty and popular government.

But before Spain was driven out of the Netherlands the British had given her a staggering blow by defeating her "Invincible Armada," which the arrogant Philip II. sent in 1588 to subjugate England. This was one of the most disastrous defeats in history; it broke the power of Spain on the sea and gave it to England, and opened the way for colonial settlements by both the Dutch and English in America.

A little later, in 1639, Spain was again humiliated by the loss of Portugal and its foreign colonies. During the latter part of the same century Spain was beaten by France and suffered a loss of eight million more in her population. Another war (1701–1714) pared away what was left of the great Spanish Empire on every side; Gibraltar and the island of Minorca were ceded to England; Milan, Naples, Sardinia, and Belgium were given to Austria. From the mightiest nation in Europe, Spain thus sank in a little over a hundred years to a third-rate power. But she still held a lordly empire over the seas in the Western Hemisphere.

From that opulent American empire she had drawn her treasure for her extravagant and foolish wars at home. She had made the American natives slaves, and had, by harsh treatment, exterminated whole races of them. She might have learned some valuable lessons from her own terrible reverses in Europe and instituted a milder and juster sway in America. But her

Rulers and Leaders of Spain.

King Alfonso XIII. and his Mother, the Queen-Regent.
Captain-General Weyler.   Prime Minister Sagasta.

misrule and extortion grew heavier in her colonies, and they steadily slipped away from her.

Accordingly, by the time another century had passed, Spain began to lose her vast American empire. Stimulated by the success of the United States in its winning of independence, the Spanish colonies followed one another in rebellion. The Argentine Republic, including Bolivia, established its independence in 1810. Chili, Venezuela, Ecuador, and New Granada achieved theirs during the next ten years. Peru won freedom in 1824. Mexico and the states of Central America broke the Spanish yoke through bloody revolutions about the same time. Florida was bought from Spain by the United States; and the Louisiana territory, including the enormous region west of the Mississippi and north as far as the British possessions, after having been ceded by Spain to France, came to us soon afterwards through diplomacy and purchase from France.

Brazil had gone when Portugal was lost. Santo Domingo and Hayti, which had been gradually conquered by the French, won their independence. Jamaica and the Bahama Islands were taken by the British.

In the West Indies, accordingly, Cuba and Puerto Rico were the only islands of importance left under the Spanish rule at the beginning of the late war.

The great and rich islands of the East India group in the Pacific were properly claimed by Spain through the discoveries by Magellan; but all save the Philippines, the Carolines, the Ladrones, and a few other very small islands were taken from her by the English,

French, and Dutch in the wars she had waged against those countries in the vain hope of broadening her empire.

It would have been no dishonor to lose all of these vast possessions, had not most of the losses been occasioned by dishonest dealings, signal violations of human rights, and merciless cruelty. An habitual disregard of the customs of civilized administration and of the laws of civilized warfare has persistently formed the substance of Spanish policy. It was so in the home country and it has invariably been so in the territories.

The details of the persecution of the men and women who thought for themselves, the narrative of the expulsion of the Jews and the Moors from Spain, and the tale of the atrocities of the war in the Netherlands, are too long and too horrible to be described. We should willingly pass them by without mention if similar practices had not been brought to the New World and continued into the present century.

During the religious wars of France in the latter half of the 16th century, several hundred Huguenots, aided by Admiral Coligny, started a colony in Florida. It was the first attempt in America to establish a free government, where men could enjoy liberty of opinion. The famous English Admiral Hawkins visited this colony in 1565, became deeply interested in it, and has left a description of its broad and humane policy, which was extraordinary for that day. Shortly after Hawkins left, the terrible Menendez, with his Spanish soldiers, arrived, and butchered the whole company of

men, women, and children, seven hundred in all, except six who escaped to an English ship.

Spanish official documents show that when Venezuela, Ecuador, and New Granada battled for freedom,
eighty thousand of their people, taken prisoners of
war, were hanged, shot, or otherwise murdered in
cold blood by Spanish soldiers.   Frequently these
massacres were in spite of express agreements before
capitulation that their lives and property should be
secure.   These crimes were not due merely to the
excesses of half-savage troops, but had the specific
approval of the Government of Spain.

Special hostility was shown against people who could
read and write, and particularly against all who were
accomplished as scholars, on the ground that they
" were more dangerous than insurgents in arms."

In the city of Guanaxuato, in Mexico, men and
women who pass a certain point in the public square
still stop and cross themselves.   It is where a Spanish
general slaughtered thousands of defenseless men and
women because they were asking for freedom; and he
was rewarded for doing it by promotion to the highest
office in the territory.

In the Mexican Revolution, in June, 1816, the little
fort of Soto la Marina, after being bravely defended,
was obliged to surrender to Spanish arms.   Written
articles of capitulation were agreed upon, and they were
so similar to the terms granted by General Shafter to
the Spanish garrison at Santiago that they are worth
quoting: " I. All parties composing the garrison of

the fort of Soto la Marina, as well as those that are or
may have been at the bar or on the river, shall be
included in the present capitulation. They shall surrender themselves prisoners of war, everyone receiving a treatment corresponding with his rank; and the
officers shall be paroled. II. All private property
shall be respected. III. The foreigners shall be sent
to the United States, by the first opportunity. The
natives of the country shall be sent to their respective
homes, and their past conduct shall remain wholly un-
noticed. IV. The garrison shall march out with the
honors of war, and stack their arms." Notwithstanding this solemn agreement, most of the garrison were
murdered, and such as were not shot were sent to end
their lives in dungeons, a few in Mexico and the rest
in Spain. The property of all was confiscated.

In the same revolution, in January, 1818, the Mexi-
cans surrendered the fort of Los Remedios. Here,
too, the garrison was slaughtered, and the captors were
not content with shooting such as were well, but they
fired the hospital, which was filled with sick and
wounded, and as the poor unfortunates crawled out
they were thrust back into the flames or put to death
with bayonets.

There seems to be no end to the story of these brutali-
ties. They have occurred for more than four hundred
years at times when the Spanish soldiers have won the
victory in battle. Four centuries ago all nations were
shockingly cruel as compared with the present stand-
ards, but the Spaniards at that time exceeded all other

peoples in mercilessness; and while other nations have grown humane and gentle with the advance of better civilization, the Spaniards have lagged behind, and have continued to hold sentiments so savage as often to impel them to war against helpless prisoners, women, and children with the same ferocity with which they fight against soldiers in arms. Consequently terrible assassinations and massacres have usually followed Spanish conquest. They have not been repressed, but rather encouraged and approved, by the Spanish Government.

It is not pleasant to tell this story, but it is a part of the world's history, it bears upon the course of the United States concerning the Spaniards, and it has at last settled the fate of Spain.

CHAPTER II

Spanish Misrule in Cuba

THE island of Cuba was the chief discovery made by Columbus upon his first voyage. Passing by several smaller islands, he came to this one and supposed he had reached the main coast of China, the far-famed " Indie " of that day. He wrote in his diary, " This is the most beautiful land ever beheld by human eyes." The Spaniards have called it, at different times, Juana, Fernandino, Santiago, and Ave Maria, but " Cuba," the name by which the original inhabitants called it, has survived all others.

The length of Cuba is about 700 miles; it has an irregular width which varies from 21 to 111 miles; with several small islands along the coast, it contains about 47,000 square miles. What this means is suggested by a comparison. Cuba is nearly one fourth larger than Ireland, and nearly one seventh smaller than England. It is a trifle larger than Virginia or Ohio, and a trifle smaller than Pennsylvania. It has 2200 miles of coast-line. Its population in recent years has probably been about 1,600,000, of whom 950,000 were white Cubans, 500,000 colored, and the rest Spaniards.

Perhaps no other place on earth has a more genial

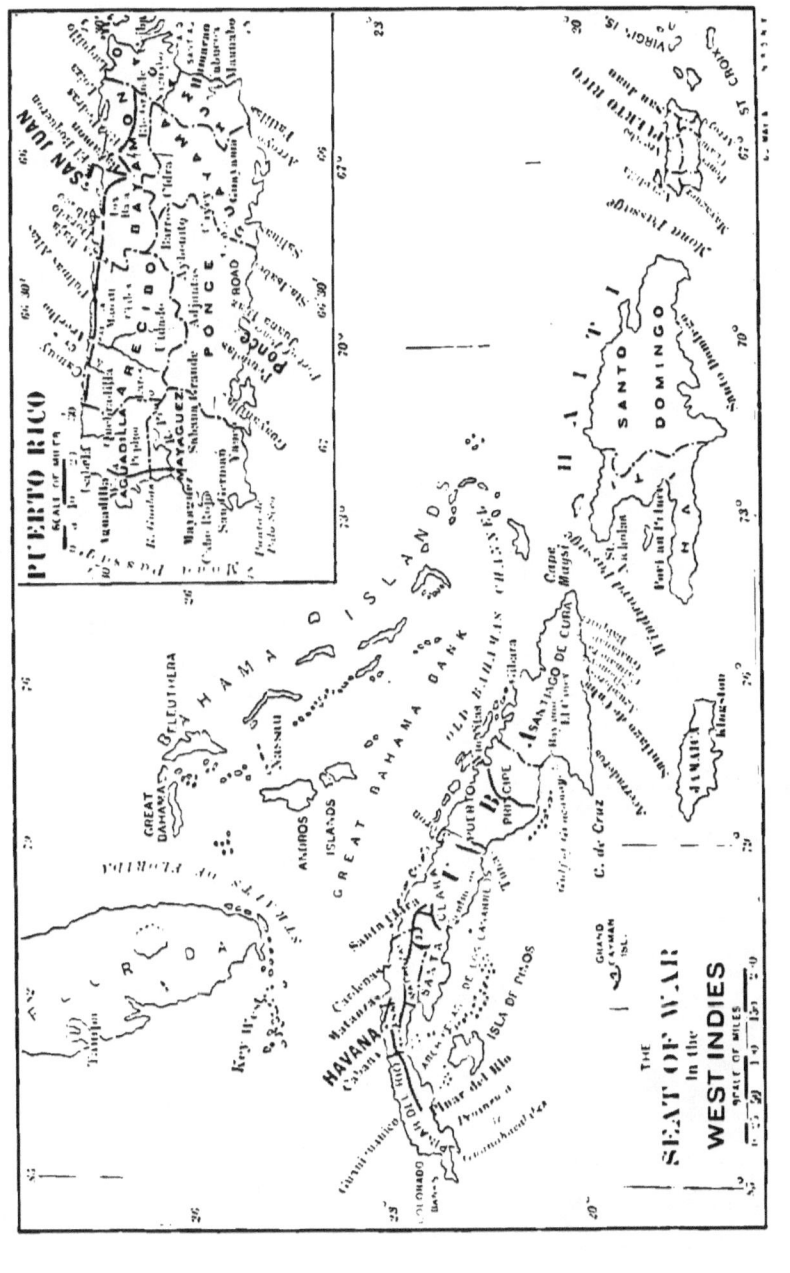

climate, vegetation more thriving and beautiful, or fruit more delicious and abundant. The temperature ranges from 50° to 88°. Thirteen million acres of uncleared and virgin forest contain the finest cedar and mahogany in the world. Two million acres of the island's thirty-four millions are under cultivation, and nine millions are natural pasture-land. The most important products of the soil are sugar, tobacco, Indian corn, coffee, cocoa, bananas, pineapples, and cocoanuts, besides the rich woods of the forest and the copper and iron from the mines.

Even in the war year of 1896 the total exports amounted to over $94,000,000. Until laid waste by war Cuba was thus a treasure-house for Spain, and it is no wonder that she was unwilling to give up so rich a spot of earth.

From the beginning the history of the island has been that of bloodshed and oppression. The poor natives at first believed that their discoverers had descended from heaven, but they were soon disabused of this idea. Though discovered by Columbus in 1492, the conquest of the island was not undertaken seriously by the Spaniards until 1511. The island was divided among the conquerors and the Indians were made slaves to till the land. But so ruthless were their taskmasters that in a few centuries almost the whole native population of the island had disappeared. Then negroes were imported from Africa to take their places.

For the next three centuries Cuba was left by her oppressors to isolation and neglect. Her people lived

in poverty and squalor. With extraordinary short-
sightedness the Government of Spain took no steps
towards the development of the country or the well-
being of the people.

Her centralized and inefficient administration, influ-
enced by an unprogressive spirit of routine, has always
looked upon proposed reforms as dangerous experiments. Whenever a new industry was started through
private enterprise, the Government demanded a new
tax, which was made heavier as the industry developed.
The first important industry was tobacco: Spain immediately so taxed and monopolized its culture, sale,
and manufacture that the planters in desperation several
times rose in arms and destroyed their fields, rather
than to submit to exactions which more than deprived
them of their profits.

The English captured Havana in 1762. During the
British occupation the port was thrown open to foreign
trade for the first time, and the inhabitants had the
experience of its advantages. A desire for education
began to be felt; and, there being no institutions in the
country which could satisfy it, a few young men were
sent to the United States for schooling. But Spain
did not approve of education. A royal decree was
issued in Madrid in 1799 that Cuban parents should be
dissuaded from continuing a practice from which they
were told only evil consequences could be expected!
All Cuban youths in school in the United States were
ordered back to Cuba, while those who had received an
education were placed under the watch of the police.

Revolts against these injustices at last began; the first was in 1823, and was followed by others in 1826, 1828, 1830, 1848, 1850, 1851, and 1855; then came the great " ten years' war " of 1868–78, after which there was an apparent peace until the last revolution, which began in 1895.

In the earlier times all the European nations were accustomed to look upon their colonial dependencies as sources of support for the home Government, and often as the legitimate objects of plunder for the home people. England learned a most useful lesson as to this kind of dealing when one of her political administrations, under a king who was either crazy or simple, pursued a course which forced the Americans into their Revolution, and thus she lost her best possessions across the Atlantic. It was a course which ever since has been deeply regretted by the British statesmen and the body of the English people. Great Britain has learned to administer her colonies for their benefit rather than her own, and has found that by so doing she added to the greatness of her empire.

Spain, on the other hand, has suffered a more bitter experience in the loss of colonies than any other nation, but she has seemed incapable of profiting by experience. One by one, her vast American possessions, from Mexico to Patagonia, revolted against her; but as these dependencies slipped away her dealings with those that remained grew but little less severe and reckless. Her colonial policy continued to be wholly for the home country, with but scanty regard for the rights and interests of the colonists. She permitted them no government of their own, nor even effective representation in the Madrid Government, although she promised it more than once. She held them down by military force. She sent to them governors whose dishonest rule was unbearable. She taxed them beyond endurance, while her officials grew rich through unarrested corruption. Puerto Rico and the Philippines suffered similarly with Cuba; yet it seemed as if poor Cuba, because of her frequent revolts against the tyranny, as well as because of her superior wealth, was singled out for a special rigor.

The " ten years' war " cost nearly a billion of dollars,—and Cuba was required to pay it. That war was concluded by the promises of the Spanish Government, on its word of honor, to accord various important reforms; most of these Spain never granted. Before the outbreak of the last revolution, in 1895, the debt which Spain had put upon the unhappy island was $295,707,264. This debt meant $185 to each inhabitant. The United States debt before 1898 meant only $24 to each person. Even the gigantic debt of France, which she incurred herself, means only $154 to each person. Before her last revolution began, Cuba's debt signified more to each inhabitant than any other debt in the world. Yet this debt was not only imposed by Spain without a word of consent from Cuba; the money had all been spent for Spain. It was declared by the revolutionary Cubans that this enormous sum " had not contributed to build a single kilometer of highway,

nor had it built one asylum or opened one public
school." What had not been embezzled, had gone
chiefly to pay Spain's expense in keeping Cuba under
her inflexible rule.

The interest on this prodigious debt was $12,000,-
000, which Spain required Cuba to pay. She also imposed upon the island an annual payment of $7,000,000
to support the army and navy kept there for Cuba's
own repression; and $8,000,000 more for the salaries
and expenses of the civil, judicial, and other officers
of Spain; and to all this we must add a sum of from
$12,000,000 to $20,000,000, which the best informed
men say was lost to the Cuban revenue through the
purloining of officials, and had to be made good by the
suffering people.

In the general yearly expenditure of about $34,000,-
000, the accounts showed that only $500,000 were
devoted to works of public utility, and $182,000 to
education. Yet the people who endured this monstrous
wrong were less in number than in many American
States. They were mostly poor, and of course they
were illiterate, for the trifle which was spent upon
education did not apply to any except the privileged
classes. They were without voice or vote concerning
the taxes that were exacted, and saw no return for
them in the way of public improvements. How would
the people of an American State regard official misrule
and exaction to this extent ?

As to personal rights, there was even less of constitutional freedom in the island than in Spain herself.

3

The Governor-General ruled with unlimited powers; he had the general authority of an autocratic sovereign. At his caprice, and without trial, he could imprison persons, deport them to penal colonies, or order them to be shot; he could then confiscate their estates and reduce their families to want. It has been said that there is hardly a Cuban family in which one of the members has not suffered persecution during the last seventy years. If one ventured from home without a Government license, costing from twenty-five cents to fifty dollars, according to his means, he could be arrested. There was no real liberty of thought or action. Public meetings could not be held without the permission of the Spanish authorities, and when they were allowed an officer was present to stop them if anything was said which he did not like. It was the policy of the Government to break the spirit of the whole Cuban people, and so to strip them of their means that they could not successfully revolt.

But under these conditions they could do nothing less than revolt. The last Cuban rebellion broke out in 1895. It bore evidence of being more intelligently and effectually organized than any which had preceded it. Strong and experienced men planned and led it. Gomez, the two Maceos, Garcia, and others were noted patriots as well as men of high ability.

The system of raising money for the Army of Liberation extended to all who naturally would sympathize with it. Every patriotic Cuban, rich and poor, gave as he was able, and those who could give nothing else

gave themselves to the patriot army, which fought without pay and often without food. When the army was without arms and ammunition, as often happened, it eluded the Spanish columns, and the men scattered, to return later to an appointed rendezvous. Whenever able, it made sudden attacks on Spanish garrisons or upon the marching Spanish columns. The Cuban army could not fight great battles, because there never were enough arms to equip a large force at one time; but the harassing attacks of the small bodies of patriots were so audacious and frequent that the Spanish officers despaired of reducing the rebellion by any other means than starvation.

Consequently, in her extremity Spain resorted to barbarous measures for the suppression of the rebellion. It was believed in Madrid that Governor-General Campos was too mild for the emergency; so General Weyler was sent to take his place. Weyler already had a record for unexceeded mercilessness, and was popularly known as " the butcher." He straightway instituted new methods, which were based upon the deliberate purpose of making Cuba such a desert that the Cuban army could not obtain the least subsistence.

In pursuance of this plan he ordered his soldiers to burn the buildings and the ripening crops on all the estates. All the farming population throughout the island were driven from their homes by his guerrillas, and were gathered in the heavily garrisoned cities, where they were huddled within great pens called " trochas." These expulsions, and the long marches of the weary and fainting people from their homes to the distant garrisons, were so pitiful as to stir the hearts of all except the most incorrigible.

It became a war not only upon men, but also upon women and children. Its horrors seemed to bring back the days of Cortez in Mexico and Pizarro in Peru. The Spanish soldiers, exasperated by the lack of success in the field against the armed patriots, attacked hospitals and murdered the wounded and sick, just as in July, 1898, their sharpshooters around Santiago shot the wounded American soldiers.

When residents of Cuba, loyal to Spain, protested against these outrages they were considered to be traitors and were also shot.

These things are not from the history of the Duke of Alva in the Netherlands; they occurred in 1896 and 1897, almost within sight of the United States.

While the Spanish soldiers were perpetrating these deeds, General Weyler was declaring to his Government that Cuba was almost pacified; he was making it a desert and calling it peace.

Of course the Spanish denied many of the reports of personal outrages which were sent from Cuba by American and English observers. But there was no attempt to deny the sufferings of hundreds of thousands of the poor " reconcentrados," as the people driven from their homes to the cities by the soldiers were called; their beggary, and their starving to death in the streets of the cities, where they had been driven as into prison-pens, were too evident.

Senator Proctor of Vermont, who went to Cuba early in 1898, to satisfy himself of what was being done, addressed the Senate of the United States upon the subject. The character of the man and the deliberation with which he spoke carried conviction to the country. A few sentences from this address must suffice, but they are full of meaning.

He said: " I saw no house or hut for four hundred miles of railroad. . . . They had lived in cabins made of palms, or in wooden houses. Some of them had houses of stone, the blackened walls of which are all that remain to show that the country was ever inhabited. . . . In the trochas they were allowed to build huts of palm-leaves. They have no floor but the ground, no furniture, and but little clothing.

" The commonest sanitary provisions are impossible. Conditions are unmentionable in this respect. With foul earth, foul air, foul water, and foul food or none, it is not strange that one half have died and that one quarter of the living are now so diseased that they cannot be saved.

" Little children are walking about with arms and chests terribly emaciated, eyes swollen, and abdomen bloated to three times the natural size. The physicians say their cases are hopeless. . . . Deaths in the street have not been uncommon. . . . They have been found dead about the markets in the morning, where they have crawled in the hope of getting some stray bits of food.

" These people were independent and self-support-

ing before. . . . They have not learned the art of
begging. Rarely is a hand held out to you for alms
when going among their huts, but the sight of them
makes an appeal stronger than words.

"I saw a hospital in Havana where four hundred
women and children were lying on stone floors in an
indescribable state of emaciation and disease, many
with the scantiest covering of rags,—and such rags!

"And the conditions in other cities were even
worse. . . . *Two hundred thousand* have died within
these Spanish prison walls within a few months."

It is unnecessary to extend the details of the distress-
ing narrative: it is the story of men but half clothed
and half fed, ignorant and simple, fighting in the
bushes for freedom; their wives and children dead or
dying of starvation and abuse; their fields untilled and
their homes in ruins; the whole of their beautiful
island laid desolate; the future as dark as an eternal
night; yet refusing all overtures, and pressing on
without hesitation either to victory or else to utter
extermination.

Much has been said against the Cubans to show that
they are incapable of self-government. Many of these
charges are true. They are poor; they are ignorant,
not more than one tenth having received any education
at all; they are not accustomed to manage their own
affairs; they have had no chance; they have been
without schools; no high ideals have been held up to
them; they have been robbed of their property and
their freedom and their self-respect by a blind Govern-

Spanish Soldiers Driving in the Reconcentrados.

ment and a brutal soldiery.   But there is abundant
proof of their devotion, their ability, and their bravery
in the fact that for three years they fought more than
200,000 Spanish troops so successfully as to prove to
the world that they could not be subjugated.   This
was while their homes were laid in ashes and their
wives and children were starving.

Such was the situation in Cuba when the Republic
of the United States lifted up its voice among the
nations and declared that the oppressed island at its
doors should go free.

CHAPTER III

Rescue by the United States

TWO declarations by two presidents of the United States, in regard to the foreign policy which our Government ought to follow, have been so generally accepted by the people as to gain about as much force as a provision in the Constitution. One of these is against our meddling in the affairs of foreign nations, and the other is against allowing them to meddle in our affairs.

In the most important suggestion of his " Farewell Address "—and the only one which is commonly remembered—President Washington impressively recommended that we entirely abstain from interfering in European affairs. This advice has been uniformly followed. Even under severe temptation we have never gone further into any foreign issue than to protect our own independence and to insure the development of free institutions upon this Western Continent.

While, on several occasions in the past, our navy has been sent into foreign waters to enforce certain demands of the United States, those demands have always been made necessary by some menace to our interests or by some defiance of the legitimate authority of the United States. Until Commodore Dewey sailed from Hong Kong for Manila, no vessel of the

United States ever went over seas upon a warlike
errand which was not inseparably associated with
American rights.   The doctrine that we should mind
our own business, and that our business was all within
the bounds of the Western Continent, has been thoroughly fixed in the thought of the people, and as
firmly established in the diplomatic policy of the Government.   The last words of Washington to this effect
have always been regarded as very wise and entirely
sacred.

President Monroe, in 1823, connected his name with
the converse of this doctrine, that we should not permit European nations to interfere in our affairs, or to
extend monarchical rule, or to offer any menace to
democratic government upon this hemisphere.

It may be interesting to recall how this "Monroe
Doctrine" came to be announced.   It must be remembered that it was the efforts of Spain to reclaim
her South American colonies that called it forth.
Following the Napoleonic wars there was formed
among the leading European nations an alliance for
self-protection.   It was called the "Holy Alliance,"
though it was anything but holy.   It was not so
much for resistance against other powers as to protect
its members against internal rebellions.   It consisted
of a joining of forces by the kings to prevent the progress of the people towards the management of their
own affairs.   England at first approved, but soon re-
pudiated the whole arrangement.

It was the attempts of Spain to bring the guns of

these allied powers to bear upon her revolted colonies in South America that led President Monroe to declare that while the United States would not interfere with any existing dependencies of any European state, yet the United States would consider it an unfriendly act, and treat it as such, for any European power to interfere with any American Government which had declared and maintained its independence and had been so recognized by the United States. In words full of meaning and bristling with spirit he said: " It is due to candor that we should declare to the Allied Powers that we should consider any attempt on their part to extend their system to any portion of this hemisphere as dangerous to our peace and safety."

So it had become a traditional and fundamental doctrine in this country that we should avoid all foreign entanglements; that we should not meddle with the affairs of foreign nations, even with the affairs of their American colonies; and that, on the other hand, we should not allow them to extend their monarchical systems on this side of the Atlantic.

The decision of our Government to intervene in behalf of Cuba was, accordingly, a complete departure from traditional understandings. Some of the foremost constitutional lawyers were opposed to it. The step was disapproved by a large proportion of the professional and business people of the country: *it was forced by the masses*. It was the impulses of human sympathy and righteous indignation setting aside the long-standing principles of national policy.

Various things had contributed to arouse American sentiment against Spain. Her whole history was not only opposed to our manner of living and our common thought, but she had done some things which bore directly against American citizens and gave a serious wound to American feelings.

In 1873, the steamer Virginius, flying the American flag and suspected of carrying supplies to the Cubans, then engaged in revolt against Spain, was captured by a Spanish cruiser and taken into the harbor of Santiago. Her officers and crew, to the number of fifty-three, were taken hurriedly into the public square and shot. The diplomatists smoothed matters out so as to avoid war, but twenty-five years were by no means long enough to cause the outrage to be forgotten.

Furthermore, the recent revolutionary condition of the island had affected some American commercial interests; this, however, did not have wide influence upon the people, and Spain was careful to refrain from further outrages upon citizens of the United States, in order to afford no ground, recognized by the law of nations, which would be sufficient to justify our interference.

More wide-reaching was the work of the Cuban "Junta," an organization which the Cubans maintained in the United States for the purpose of distributing information concerning the revolution and arousing sympathy with their cause.

More effective still was the diligent labor of many American newspapers in constantly presenting the hard facts of Spanish savagery to their readers.

Through these means the people were increasingly agitated; yet a good many often questioned whether the " Junta " was not composed of professional agitators working for selfish ends, and whether the newspapers were not printing exaggerated stories to promote newspaper circulation.

But on the evening of the 15th of February, 1898, an incident occurred in the harbor of Havana which suddenly wrought our people to madness, which necessarily turned on the search-lights of official investigation, and led directly to a new and momentous step in the international relations of the world. It was the explosion which destroyed the battleship Maine.

Our consuls in Cuba had presented to the Government the advisability of sending an American battleship to Havana, in a friendly spirit, on the ground that the presence of our flag would restrain the combatants so far as American interests were concerned, and might aid in relaxing the strained relations which were continually increasing between our Government and that of Spain. Accordingly, after consultation with the Spanish Minister at Washington, and notice to the Government at Madrid, on the 24th of January, 1898, the Maine was ordered to pay a friendly and official visit to the harbor of Havana. She arrived on the 25th, was received with the usual naval courtesies and conducted to a place in the harbor by the Spanish pilot. She lay there without special incident for three weeks. At eight o'clock on the evening of the 15th of February all was reported secure to Captain Sigsbee,

President McKinley and Famous Officials.

Secretary of the Navy, John D. Long.   Secretary of War, Russell A. Alger.
Minister to Spain, Stewart L. Woodford.   Consul-General in Cuba, Fitzhugh Lee.

her commander.   At forty minutes after nine the vessel was lifted from the water by two terrific explosions and quickly sank, carrying to watery graves two of her officers and two hundred and sixty-four members of her crew.

The cause of the disaster was a mystery, but American sentiment was not slow in attributing it to Spanish treachery.   The Captain-General and other officials at Havana disavowed all knowledge and tendered their sympathy, and the Government at Madrid hastened to express its regrets, but the people of the United States recalled the interminable line of Spanish intrigue, and were impatient of the various specious theories which excused the Spaniards from responsibility.   If the explosion was not caused directly by Spanish authority, our people were convinced it had been caused at least by Spanish officers who had access to the mines and torpedoes, and who were protected and hidden by their military superiors.

Nevertheless, self-restraint prevailed.   Captain Sigsbee, in announcing the explosion, had said, " Suspend judgment "; and the temper of the people and of Congress was in accord with this very sensible advice during the long weeks while our Naval Board of Inquiry, which had been appointed immediately after the disaster, were investigating, with the greatest care, the cause of the explosion.

But though judgment was suspended the country was seething with excitement.   The flag suddenly began to float from nearly every building.   The schools and churches seemed to throb with patriotism. Night after night the wildest cheering greeted the playing of the patriotic airs in the theaters and cafés. Audiences everywhere arose to their feet while " The Star-Spangled Banner " was played. There had been nothing like this universal stirring of the spirit of the country since 1861.

Meanwhile the lights were being turned, full force, on all the doings of Spain in Cuba, and the conviction grew that the former newspaper reports of Spanish inhumanity, which many people had considered exaggerated, had not depicted things as bad as they really were.

For one thing, it was discovered that there were, locked up in the files of the State Department, facts of the most startling nature regarding the Cuban conflict which had been reported by our consuls to the preceding Administration, and which, in the interests of peace, it had been deemed advisable to withhold from the public. These earlier reports, and the later ones received from Consul-General Fitzhugh Lee, showed the condition of the poor Cubans who had been driven from their farms and concentrated in the fortified cities without means of subsistence, to have grown steadily more horrible. Here is a sample report concerning the " reconcentrados " in Santa Clara:

" It was there shown that while there were 5,489 deaths in that town in the seven years previous to 1897, which included 1,417 in one year from an epidemic of yellow fever, there were, owing to the concentration order, 6,981 deaths out of a total population of 14,000 in the year 1897 alone. The death-rate increased monthly from 78 in January, the month before the concentration order went into effect, until December, when there were 1,011 deaths.''

Several congressmen visited Cuba to see for themselves. The speeches in Congress of Senators Proctor, of Vermont, and Thurston, of Nebraska, during this period of suspense, were perhaps almost as influential as the destruction of the Maine in deepening the public demand that Spain be driven from this hemisphere. Senator Proctor's speech, already referred to, was very judicial, but the horrors that he described in his extremely guarded way seemed the more terrible for his self-restraint. Senator Thurston's wife had accompanied him to Cuba, and the shock caused by the unspeakable sufferings of the '' reconcentrados '' had killed her. When the Senator, upon his return to the Senate, arose to speak of Spanish inhumanity, he poured forth a flood of anguished invective which moved the heart of the public not less than Senator Proctor's measured statements.

When the appalling facts thus became known to a certainty—the hard fighting, the intense suffering, the abuse of prisoners; particularly, when it was known that hundreds of thousands of women and children from the rural districts had already starved through the ruthless course of the Spanish Captain-General,—and all because of a desire for liberty,—the public sympathy and indignation in the United States, so long restrained, were ready to break all bonds.

3

But while Congress and perhaps most of the people were calling for war, the President and his advisers were engaged in the twofold effort of diligently preparing for war and earnestly working for peace.

President McKinley, who had himself been through the horrors of one war, did everything in his power to avert the coming conflict. In his inaugural message he had said: "We have cherished the policy of non-interference with the affairs of foreign Governments wisely inaugurated by Washington, keeping ourselves from entanglements either as allies or foes. We want no wars of conquest. We must avoid the temptation of territorial aggression. War should never be entered upon until every agency of peace has failed."

The resources of diplomacy were pressed by the President until they were exhausted, in endeavors to induce Spain to cease hostilities and withdraw from Cuba.

Members of Congress who were most eager for war were urged by the President to aid him in holding back the rush into armed conflict. It was believed by many of the wisest of our statesmen that through diplomacy Spain might be induced to acknowledge herself defeated in Cuba, and to leave the island to itself. As the Great Powers of Europe saw the conflict approaching, their diplomatists at Washington and Madrid were instructed to use their best offices to avert the final clash.

With no less diligence, however, was the President preparing the national forces for the struggle if it must come. Our defenses were in a deplorable state of neglect; coast fortifications were notoriously unprepared to resist an attack. Our navy, though well equipped, and in a high state of discipline, was nevertheless, in fighting ships, considered to be somewhat weaker than that of Spain.

The President, therefore, on the 8th of March, requested from Congress an appropriation of fifty million dollars for the national defense. This was immediately voted without a dissenting voice. It was hoped that this spectacle of unanimous support given to the President in the demands he was making upon Spain, and the suggestion it contained of the unlimited wealth of the nation, might convince Spain of the hopelessness of war with the United States. The President at once made use of this most needed money to strengthen our coast fortifications, to buy military equipments of all kinds, and to enlarge the navy as rapidly as possible by the purchase of more ships.

The whole world was searched by our agents to find warships belonging to other nations which might be for sale. The Spanish were doing the same thing; yet we were able to buy a few warships. By leasing and by purchase an immense auxiliary fleet of cruisers, transports, yachts, and tugs was pressed into the service of the Government, and a patrol of picket vessels was established the entire length of our Atlantic coast.

Meantime, the Naval Board of Inquiry sent its report from Havana. It was received by the President on the 25th of March, and was given to Congress on the 28th of March. It found that the Maine had been sunk by an *explosion from the outside*. Though it would not attribute this explosion to the hostile act of the Government of Spain, the fact was palpable that a Spanish torpedo had wrought the disaster, and that the Spaniards had made no efforts to discover the culprits.

Even yet, however, the President did not despair of peace, and was unwilling as yet to make the destruction of the Maine a cause of war. More efforts were made to induce the Spanish Government to withdraw from Cuba. But finally President McKinley sent a message to Congress on the 11th of April, in which he recited the inhuman practices of the Spanish authorities in Cuba, and mentioned the destruction of the Maine as an instance of Spanish inability to restrain misrule; in view of all the facts the President stated to Congress his belief that forcible interference between Cuba and Spain was now justified. Congress immediately responded, and on the 19th of April—the anniversary of the battles of Lexington and Concord—passed a declaration of war which, when finally concurred in, was in the following words:

" First. That the people of the island of Cuba are, and of right ought to be, free and independent.

" Second. That it is the duty of the United States to demand, and the Government of the United States does hereby demand, that the Government of Spain at once relinquish its authority and government in the island of Cuba and withdraw its land and naval forces from Cuba and Cuban waters.

A Group of American Major-Generals

Wesley R. Shafter.   Wesley Merritt.
                Nelson A. Miles.
John R. Brooke.   Joseph Wheeler.

" Third. That the President of the United States be, and he is hereby, directed and empowered to use the entire land and naval forces of the United States, and to call into the actual service of the United States the militia of the several States, to such extent as may be necessary to carry these resolutions into effect.

" Fourth. The United States hereby disclaims any disposition or intention to exercise sovereignty, jurisdiction, or control over said island except for the pacification thereof, and asserts its determination when that is accomplished to leave the government and control of the island to its people."

This declaration of war, in its purpose, its form, and its spirit, touches the high-water mark of government by the people for the good of mankind.

It is true that in other times strong nations have aided the weak in their battles for freedom. Queen Elizabeth of England aided the heroic Dutch to throw off the yoke of the cruel King of Spain; yet her battle against the Spaniards was more for the strengthening of her own throne and for the defense of English liberty against the danger of Spanish aggression than it was to help the Dutch.

King Louis XVI. of France sent his soldiers and his ships across the sea to aid Washington in our own American struggle for independence; but it was the desire to humble England for former defeat which moved the King of France more than his love of human liberty. The French Revolutionary Republic, a few years later, marched into Italy and liberated the oppressed nationalities there; but each battle fought by France in Italy was a blow for the defense of the young French Republic itself against the foreign despotisms which threatened it.

Surely never before has a people, aroused by the contemplation of appalling tyranny in a neighboring country and with an entire disinterestedness of spirit, declared war against the foreign oppressors and bound itself beforehand to give to the liberated people a free government of their own.

It marks a gratifying advance in the ideals of good government when a great self-governing nation, in one of the most solemn of national acts, carries, with her great heart and strong arm, the blessings of civil liberty, religious toleration, and popular education to the struggling subjects of a rapacious empire. Such an act helps the world to realize that states do not exist for the benefit of their Governments, nor even for security alone, but for the intellectual and moral progress of the people. It presents before all nations a loftier ideal, and it gives to the flag of our Republic a brighter and more glorious meaning.

CHAPTER IV

The Preparation

THE ordinary American never has any doubts of the power of his country to accomplish whatever it undertakes. If it will attempt something new and difficult he has the greater relish for it. The experienced ones may see the difficulties and plead for deliberation: the crowd will take counsel of their own enthusiasm rather than of their fears. Entire confidence that the nation will spring to any mighty effort with a bound is an American trait.

The impulses of the public, generous and soul-felt, carried the United States into the war with Spain in disregard of the national traditions, without much thought on the part of the people as to preparedness, but with the usual American confidence as to the result.

The nation was not at all prepared for war. It never has been prepared for war except in the midst of war. It has never even prepared for defense until in the immediate presence of attack. Such preparedness as it has had hitherto has been in its spirit, in its unbounded confidence that it can do anything it undertakes and do it quickly. It is not too much to say that it has had little interest in doing things as other countries do

them.   It would have been comparatively small satisfaction to the American heart to drive Spain out of
Cuba after long preparation and by slow advances.   It
was a delight to the American people to do it with
quick preparation, to do it almost upon the instant,
and to do it so completely that none could be so stupid
as not to understand.

This popular spirit is of course both childish and
unwise.   It does not accord with our real seriousness
as a nation.   We do not conduct our ordinary business
on such a haphazard principle.   It is terribly unsafe
to trust to the luck of emergency preparation in the
event of war.

For wars to-day are very different from those of the
past.   They are now far more of an exact science and
are fought with weapons and tools and enginery that
require years in making, and they call for men on sea
and land who are trained specialists.   Even in our
great Civil War it took about a year after war began
for both sides to get ready to fight; but neither side
got any advantage, for both were equally unready.
Nowadays every powerful nation, except ours, has
great numbers of expert soldiers and vast quantities of
all the materials of war ready at hand, to be used instantly.   If we had been obliged to fight Great Britain
or Russia or Germany or France, instead of Spain, our
lack of readiness might have cost us very dear.

There are no braver men for battle in the world than
Americans; but mere bravery is no match for equal
bravery with better weapons, ampler supplies, and

superior organization.   It is the duty of our Congress
and our legislatures to see that we are never again so
poorly prepared.

At the time of the declaration of war the regular
army of the United States numbered 27,532 men.
The regular army of Great Britain in time of peace
consists of about 220,000 men, of France 2,043,000, of
Germany 1,969,000, of Russia 1,145,000, of Spain
352,000.

Our little army of regular troops has much improved
in character and efficiency in recent years.   The officers, nearly all of them graduates of the Military
Academy at West Point, are liberally educated both
as professional soldiers and as men of affairs.   It is
doubtful if any army in the world has more com-
petent commanders.   With remarkably rare exceptions, the officers are men of character themselves,
and are able to see that the character of the enlisted
man has a great deal to do with his worth as a soldier.
Much more care than formerly, therefore, is given to
the standing of the enlisted men.   They must not only
be within the limits of age, eighteen to thirty, and
in perfect health, but their habits of life and moral
character must also give promise of the willing and
efficient soldier.

Everything which good leadership among the officers
can suggest is being done in our regular army to make
for the highest efficiency.   The uniform has been
adapted to afford comfort rather than to make a show.

The old-time elaborate manual of arms has given way in considerable measure to physical exercises which are calculated to develop supple, sinewy, and hardy men who can endure hardships and perform difficult deeds requiring strength and athletic skill.   Much also has been done at the army posts to give to the private soldier a substantial education, in the confidence that the more intelligent a man is, the better soldier he will make.

The regulars were consequently reasonably well ready for service when war was declared.   They were well drilled and somewhat inured to camp life and field service.   They had a fair field equipment.   They were armed with a modern weapon called the Krag-Jörgensen rifle, and they were supplied, while in the midst of the Cuban campaign, with cartridges of smokeless powder.

But the regular troops were only a handful of men, and the points in which they excelled were only those which were within the power of the professional officers of the army to develop and direct.   Congress had for years refused not only to grant any enlargement of the army, but also · to authorize such reorganization as military experience had shown to be necessary and as had been adopted in all modern European armies. Such matters relating to the army as depended either upon legislation by Congress or upon administration by civilian officers were either seriously lacking or deplorably confused.   In the Santiago campaign the transportation and supply departments almost entirely broke down under their responsibilities.

One reason why the regular army had been kept small was because there seemed to be so little for it to do. Its only active service was in suppressing Indian outbreaks, which have been growing more infrequent. It also served the purpose of enabling the officers to maintain the standard of military efficiency. In case of war it was intended to serve as a nucleus for the volunteer army, upon which it has hitherto been the custom of our Government to depend. What we should do in case of sudden war with a powerful foreign power, Congress had not thought out.

Consequently, when war was declared, the Government was obliged to depend on volunteers to fill up the army. The President issued calls for 200,000 volunteer soldiers. Five men stood ready for every place that was to be filled. Many of the best young men in the land struggled with each other for opportunity to go. In many States entire regiments of the National Guard volunteered. In some States whole regiments were enlisted, organized, and drilled, without any authority whatever, in the hope that further calls would be made, and, being organized, they would have the next chance.

In addition to the 200,000 volunteers called for by the President, Congress authorized an enlargement of the regular army from 27,000 to 62,000 men, and also the enlistment as " United States Volunteers " of 10,000 " immunes " (or men who were proof against yellow fever), 3,500 engineers, and 3,000 cavalrymen.

The famous " Rough Riders," led by Colonel Theodore Roosevelt, were part of the volunteer cavalry. The regiment of Rough Riders was one of the most notable bodies of troops ever enlisted in the United States service.   Every man was an expert and picturesque horseman.   Side by side in the ranks of this very democratic regiment were cowboys from the prairies, football men from the colleges, and hardy athletes from the wealthy clubs of the great cities.

The volunteer troops could not in the nature of things be prepared for service in a brief time as completely as the regulars.   Congress had made no provision for equipping a volunteer army, and the equipment furnished by the States was very inadequate. Much of the equipment which the States provided was either out of date or made for show rather than service. With all the riches of the country at the time of the declaration of war, there was almost an entire absence of clothing, shoes, tents, camp utensils, horses and wagons, arms and ammunition available for the active service of an army of 250,000 men anywhere, least of all in a campaign in a foreign and tropical country, mountainous and without roads, and in midsummer.

The American volunteer soldier is of course not inured to field service.   He is a man of wits and resources, capable of adapting himself to new conditions and rising to occasions; but he can hardly be expected, in three months, to carry himself like a professional, or to fight as effectually with antiquated arms as the veteran with rifles of the highest power.   But notwithstanding the disadvantages under which most of the volunteer troops worked, they pressed forward with alacrity, supported the regulars with unfailing courage, fought bravely when opportunity offered, and if the war had lasted would soon have been professional soldiers themselves.

The modern Krag-Jörgensen gun has far greater velocity, carries much farther, and is more accurate than the old Springfield rifle. Not a regiment of the State troops, which formed the bulk of the army, was equipped with this new gun, however, and the factory which made them could not turn out more than one hundred and fifty per day; at this rate it took nearly two weeks to fit out a single regiment. Many States sent arms of different types and calibers, so that they could not be served with the same ammunition.

There was also a scarcity of ammunition at the time of the declaration of war. This lack was so great that target practice had to be limited. But under the emergency appropriation of fifty million dollars, contracts were let for large quantities of ammunition, and the factories were worked night and day, making one kind for the regulars and other kinds for the volunteers, until they were fairly supplied.

The sequel proved that smokeless powder played a new and a large part in the efficiency and comparative safety of the troops. If the volunteer soldiers who fought at Santiago had been supplied with the Krag-Jörgensen rifle and smokeless powder, they would have been more destructive to the enemy; offering a less conspicuous target by their clouds of smoke, they would have suffered less slaughter themselves.

Each passing month saw more deficiencies remedied, however, and by the time we were through with the war the army was nearly prepared for a war. But it is an unpardonable wrong that brave American youth must lay down their lives in battle needlessly, or waste away with disease in camp, because of the parsimony of successive Congresses, or the inaction of State legislatures, or because ambitious politicians insist upon trying to do things which none but professional soldiers are capable of doing well.

The navy, fortunately, was better prepared for battle than the army, and the navy had to strike the first blows. The changes from a peace to a war footing in the navy are not so marked as in the army. The necessary additions to the force of men are smaller and less conspicuous. Moreover, the naval service has been saved from the political officer. Men who are certain they can lead troops on land have more hesitation about managing battleships at sea, and so the direction of the navy is in hands that are properly and thoroughly trained.

For nearly a score of years Congress had been making considerable appropriations for naval vessels. Many of these were ready for service, and they were the best upon the seas, commanded by the most thoroughly educated naval officers in the world. The science of naval architecture had been developed by

American naval officers to an extent unequaled by any other Government.

The first and largest expenditures from the special fifty million dollar appropriation, made by Congress just before the war, were in the purchase of additional vessels. Everything available, at home and abroad, which would be likely to prove effective was taken. Ocean greyhounds, ferryboats, tugs, millionaires' yachts, were brought into service. They were all put under the command of trained naval officers. Mechanical experts were brought from the technical schools, the Land-Grant colleges, and the State universities to strengthen the force of naval workers. The cadets from the Naval Academy at Annapolis were ordered to the vessels.

The militia of the Naval Reserve volunteered for service, and most of them were assigned to the auxiliary fleet. The sterling patriotism of this body of men deserves particular mention. The majority of them were amateur yachtsmen; some of them were men who owned large yachts themselves. When they volunteered, their former organization was broken up and they accepted duty on the same level with all the other jack-tars of the service. There is a much greater distance socially between the officers and men in the navy than in the army; yet these yachtsmen, when they enlisted aboard the national cruisers, accepted coal-heaving and every other humble duty without a thought of complaint, showing how deeply ingrained in the American mind is the essentially democratic feeling.

A gun factory had been established in Washington
during the last years of President Cleveland's first administration.   There enormous guns were turned out
faster than the ships to carry them could be built.
Their quality and mechanism have seemed to be perfect.   Never has an explosion occurred with one of
them through flaws in steel or faulty workmanship.

The American sailor has always been preëminent as
a marksman.   It was fine gunnery as well as seaman-
ship that had won our brilliant victories in the War of
1812.   As soon as our modern sailors found themselves
behind the wonderful guns of recent manufacture,
they set themselves to master all their possibilities.
Of no use is the highly developed gun unless it hits
the mark, and it is the American spirit to make every
machine do its best; consequently target practice has
been a constant habit of our officers and men.   Ships
have vied with one another in accuracy of marksmanship.   Since each cartridge for the heavier guns cost
more than five hundred dollars, our men invented
the process of using the intricate machinery of the
big gun with a common hand-rifle, making due allow-
ance in placing the target for the difference in carrying
power.

By constant application to all kinds of gun practice
the intelligent American sailor developed a coolness of
calculation and a fertility of device which made him
the most skilled and unfailing gunner in the world.
Notwithstanding this preëminent efficiency, as soon
as war began to seem probable our officers immediately

Four Fighting Admirals.

George Dewey.   William T. Sampson.
Winfield S. Schley.   Pascual de Cervera.

increased the amount of gun-shooting, as if they had no other object in life than proficiency as gunners.

Ships assembled in fleets in both oceans and practiced in day and night drills. Target practice, searchlight drills, attacks by torpedo boats, and their repulse by the ships catching them in their search-light meshes in time to blow them out of the water with the rapid-fire guns before they could reach the vessel, were kept up hourly until the war with Spain was declared. Consequently, when the wire flashed the news of war to the impatient ships, and our fleets swept out to sea, the navy was in a splendid state of efficiency, both in spirit and in intelligent discipline.

The purchase and equipment of the hospital ship Solace gave the American navy the first ambulance vessel in the world. Fitted with wards and operating rooms and all other modern hospital conveniences, and flying the flag of the Red Cross, she was prepared to go from vessel to vessel, take off the sick and wounded, give them adequate care, and return with them to the United States. The fortunes of war happily made her service in the Spanish war very inconsiderable to American sailors, but it is a gratification that she was able to render her service of mercy to so many sailors of Spain, turning former enemies into friends and admirers of the United States.

Of course there were some deficiencies in the navy, but fortunately they were of a kind which the exigencies of the service did not happen to make conspicuous. The worst one was the lack of dry-dock facilities.

With an extensive fleet upon the Atlantic coast, the navy has been until very recently without a dry-dock capable of accommodating the larger battleships. A year before the destruction of Cervera's fleet, the battleship Indiana had to be sent to the British dry-dock in Halifax for repairs because there was no American dock large enough to take her in. The trouble, which arose from lack of foresight and from undue economy, is being remedied now. Indeed, a month after the cessation of hostilities with Spain, a dry-dock was completed at New York capable of receiving the greatest war vessels of the world at any stage of the tide.

The matter of smokeless powder has come to be as important in the navy as in the army. Our ships were not supplied with it at Manila or Santiago. We have been behind all the first-class and even the second-class powers in putting it in use. The New Orleans, a ship bought from Brazil just before the war, had it on board when she was delivered. Our naval leaders attribute this slowness of ours to an indisposition to purchase it abroad. There are good brands of this powder in Europe, but we preferred to make it ourselves. We could manufacture smokeless powder equal to the foreign article, but it was the wish of our Government to wait until we could make a better grade than had yet been produced. The subject was very complicated and it required the highest scientific knowledge. Experiments had been going on for six years. There is no incentive like that arising from necessity and pride.

And in thirty days after the need was known to be imperative, the Government factory at Newport was turning out thousands of pounds daily, and of a quality giving greater velocity than had ever before been produced in the world.

A large degree of the readiness of the navy when war was declared, was due to the foresight and energy of the patriotic Secretary of the Navy and his able First Assistant. Secretary John D. Long, a former Governor of Massachusetts, and Assistant Secretary Theodore Roosevelt, had, since the beginning of President McKinley's administration, been working with steadfast diligence to put the naval forces of the Government in the best state of preparation which their opportunities and funds would allow. Politics had been sedulously kept out of the navy administration ; the best men had been assigned for all critical positions; the ships were where they were needed, and all the war material available had been placed in easy reach. As if the war had been foreseen, this department had done its best to prepare for it.

Taking all things together we were not more than half prepared for war when the executive officers of the Government were forced to begin hostilities by the Act of Congress. The navy was more than half prepared ; but the army was hardly prepared at all. In a few days 225,000 American citizens who had scarcely been in a camp and never seen a battle had to be organized, clothed, armed, and sent into the field.

The men, it is true, were at hand; but there was not much more of the outfit of an army ready. There were many who had misgivings. No doubt of the ultimate result was felt. No one questioned the power of the United States to conquer Spain eventually, in both the New World and the Old; but many, who knew the traditional pride of the Spanish people and the fighting qualities of the Spanish soldier, feared that it would be done only after serious reverses and at great cost.

Yet the people would not hesitate. They trusted that great resources in the hands of Anglo-Saxon intelligence and energy, and in a good cause, would give us the victory; and that each day of zealous preparation, under the pressure of the demands of battles not far off, would hasten the end and make it more overwhelming. They did not know just how the end would come, nor to what it, in turn, would lead; but, guided by sound impulses and having confidence in themselves, they were willing to wait for time to make it clear.

CHAPTER V

Dewey's Battle in Manila Bay

THE first blow delivered by the United States in behalf of Cuba was struck on the other side of the globe, in Asiatic waters; but it was so hard that it startled the nations of Europe and was heard with great satisfaction in every part of the United States.

The chief colonial possessions remaining to Spain, before this war, aside from Cuba and Puerto Rico, were the Philippine Islands. This is a group of some twelve hundred islands, about four hundred of which are inhabited, lying off the southeast coast of China. The largest one, Luzon, is about the size of the State of Kentucky. The Philippines have a population of perhaps seven million people, chiefly Malays, though many of the inhabitants have Spanish blood. The office-holders and tax-gatherers were, of course, Spaniards.

Much of the territory is fertile. The chief products are rice, sugar, coffee, tobacco, and hemp. The value of the commerce of the Philippines is estimated at more than fifty million dollars annually. The mineral deposits and lumber are considered to be exceedingly valuable, but have never been developed with modern business methods and energy.

The islands are upon the natural highways of Oriental
commerce and are of enormous commercial and military
importance, not only because of the value of their products, but also because of their safe harbors, their supplies of coal, and the relation in which they stand to
the world's trade with the unknown resources of the
vast regions embraced in the eastern countries of
Asia.

Spanish oppression, extortion, and cruelty in the
Philippines finally produced there an insurrection
scarcely less formidable than that in Cuba.   Under
the leadership of Aguinaldo, a young native somewhat
educated, thousands of the people were engaged in a
bloody warfare against the authority of Spain.   This
had led the Spaniards heavily to fortify and arm the
capital, Manila, a city with its suburbs of three hundred
thousand inhabitants, situated thirty-five miles from
the open ocean, on Manila Bay.   Forts were erected
at the entrance to the bay and an efficient army was
established in the city.   The Government arsenal and
naval station is at Cavite, on the right-hand side of the
bay as we enter, and about three quarters of the way
from the entrance to the city.

At the prospect of war with the United States, the
fortifications and the army at Manila were strengthened
and a considerable Spanish fleet gathered there.

Before the end of February, 1898, Commodore
George Dewey of the United States Navy, under instructions from the Government at Washington, began
to assemble the greater part of the American warships,

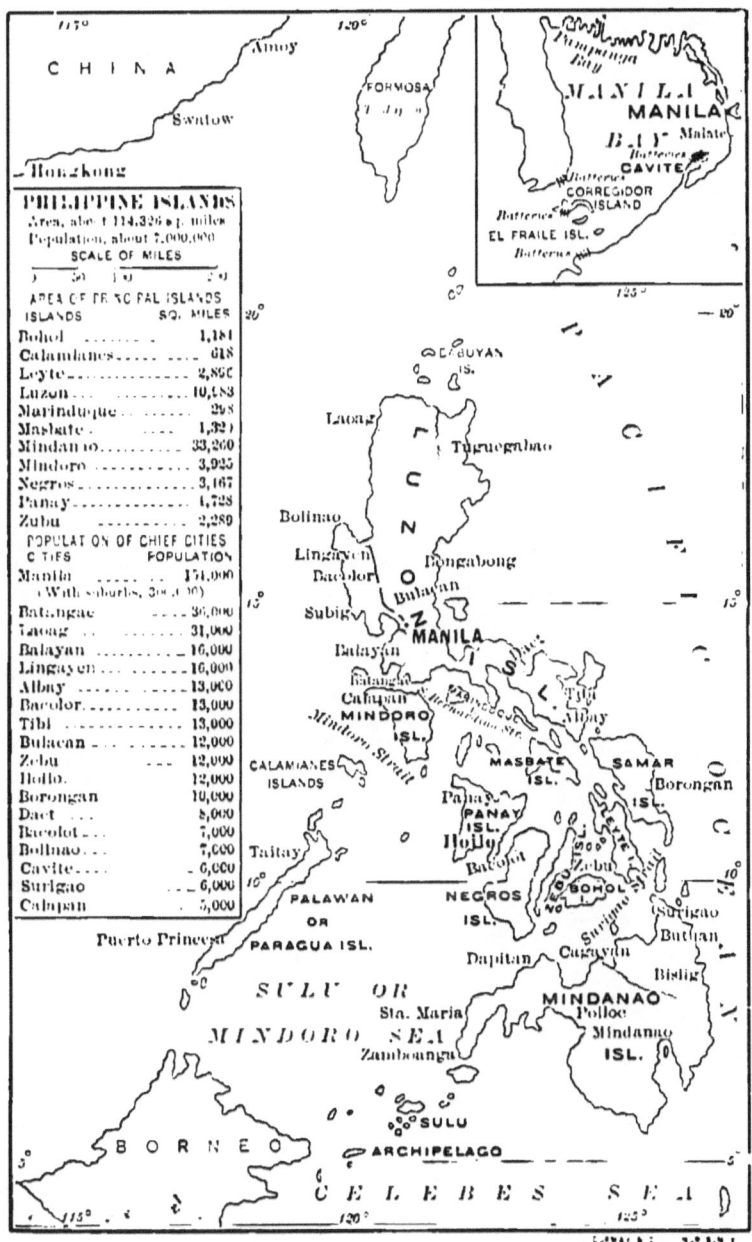

A Map of the Philippine Islands.

which were in the Pacific Ocean, at the British port of
Hong-Kong, about six hundred miles from Manila.

By the 19th of April, the day that Congress passed
its resolutions of war, the fleet consisted of the Olympia, the Boston, the Concord, the Raleigh, and the
Petrel.   On that day they began to be painted a slate
color, thus putting on their fighting uniform.   On the
22nd the Baltimore arrived from Yokohama, out of repair.   But she had no thought of losing her part in coming events, and by the end of forty-eight hours, with
the characteristic energy of our officers, she had been
put in dry-dock, scraped, repaired, painted, coaled,
provisioned, and otherwise made ready for her business.

Upon the declaration of war it became at once necessary for these vessels to leave Hong-Kong, for under
the neutrality laws, observed by all nations, when two
powers are at war the ships of either cannot harbor
with any other nation with which they are at peace.
It is said that the first notice Commodore Dewey had
that war had actually been declared came in the form
of a request from the British Foreign Office, on the
24th of April, that the fleet should leave Hong-Kong
on that account.   He replied that he would depart
from the harbor immediately.

The squadron at once got under way for Manila.   It
left Hong-Kong with bands playing and amid the
cheers of the American and English residents.   It was
accompanied by the revenue cutter Hugh McCulloch
as a dispatch boat, and two merchant vessels carrying
ten thousand tons of coal.   There were in the fleet

seventeen hundred as strong-hearted American boys
as ever sailed any sea upon a dangerous and heroic
venture.

That their errand was daring in the extreme, no one
can doubt.   The number of Spanish vessels at Manila
exceeded the number of American vessels, although in
armament and equipment there was not much difference.   The American vessels were cruisers, not battleships, as the more formidable ships of our navy are
called.   In ships of the same class we were to meet
about an equal number, and of smaller craft a larger
number; but the obvious advantage was against the
American fleet because of the forts at the mouth of
the harbor, the batteries and arsenal at Cavite, the
submerged torpedoes, and the fortifications and troops
at the city.

It was daring for another reason.   The officers of
the American fleet had never been in that harbor before.   The result was not only much in doubt, but
every man believed he had reason to expect that, if
the battle were lost, the Spanish would do by any
American prisoners as they had done very commonly by prisoners of war,—either massacre them instantly, or else, with more ceremony, take them into
the public square of the city and shoot them there.
But hearts were strong and buoyant, and eyes followed the flag as every man thought of the far-away
home and moved on to duty and to fame.

The voyage to Manila was uneventful, but each
day preparations for battle went steadily forward.

Gun drills were maintained, and once or twice in the middle of the night the blare of the bugles and the flashing of red and white signal lights called quickly upon the fleet to " clear for action." Each crew sprang to quarters and the entire fleet was put in readiness for battle. The captains reported to the Commodore that every man was at his place and every gun ready for action inside of seven minutes from the time when the crews were soundly sleeping. At evening time the bands played patriotic airs, and as they came to " Yankee Doodle " and " The Star-Spangled Banner," the men sang the words with a feeling which gave confidence in approaching victory.

On Saturday morning, the 30th of April, they were in sight of the island of Luzon. Everyone was astir, the decks were sanded, and all unnecessary material which might take fire in battle was tossed to the waves. No sight of the enemy's ships was caught that day, but it was made certain that they were harboring in the calm waters, behind the forts, the arsenal, and the submarine mines of Manila Bay. At five o'clock in the afternoon the commanders were called on board the flagship, the Olympia, for consultation with the commander-in-chief and for final orders.

The hour of twelve, midnight, was fixed for passing the forts at the entrance to the harbor in order to be ready for an engagement at daylight. The problem was to find the enemy just at daybreak and not before. The early part of the night was cloudy and dark. No lights were allowed save one at the stern of each ves-

sel, covered at the front and two sides, for the guidance
of the ship which was following, and no word was
to be spoken or movement made unless by the orders
of the commanders.   At eleven o'clock the crews were
called to quarters to be ready for any emergency, and
at midnight the ships, in single column, the flagship
leading, commenced the perilous passage.

The forts at the entrance to the bay are upon Cor-
regidor Island, six hundred feet above the water level,
and at El Fraile on the opposite side.   The channel
on one side is one mile and that on the other side five
miles wide.   The entrance was made by the wider
channel and between the forts.

As the fleet passed the island a rocket flashed from
the fort on the hill and was answered apparently by
lights on the shore.   It was supposed that this would
be followed by an immediate attack from the Krupp
guns in the shore batteries, but it was not.   The ships
moved forward until opposite the second fort, on a
small island near the shore, when there was a bright
flash, the boom of a gun, and the scream of a shell
overhead; and this was followed by a second and a third.

The Raleigh, which was third in the line, replied
with a five-inch shell, and the Concord and the Boston,
coming next, each in turn opened fire.   The shells
from the shore batteries fell wide of the mark, but with
the second flash the Yankee gunners had the spot from
which they came and placed a six-inch shell so effectually that it killed an officer and forty-one men and
silenced the battery completely.

Then the fleet passed on toward the city. The night wore away quietly and slowly. Towards morning the moon broke through the clouds. Some of the sailors lay down at their stations and dozed. The finishing touches were put on for the great battle which was at hand. The men were once more instructed as to first aid for the injured; the decks were sanded again; the boats were covered with canvas to prevent their being splintered by flying shell; the ammunition hoists were wound with cable-chains; wood partitions were torn out and thrown overboard; all impediments were put out of the way; everything that American wit and industry could do to get in the best possible condition for action was done.

The lights of Manila came in sight early and were kept directly in the line of progress. At dawn the fleet was about four miles from the city. At four o'clock coffee and hard-tack were served. It was Sunday morning and it was " May-day." At a quarter past five the forts on the Manila shore and on the shore opposite, at Cavite, fired some shots, but their shells fell a full mile from the fleet. No reply was made. The man on the bridge of the flagship had his plan and was not to be diverted from it. The dispatch boat McCulloch and the transports stopped in the middle of the bay. The cruisers passed on in single file even beyond the city, and then swung around to the right, and, under full steam, made straight for the arsenal at Cavite and for the Spanish fleet which was anchored there.

By this time the fire from the forts and the Spanish vessels, each with great battle-flags of red and gold aloft, was continuous; but the shells fell short. The American gunners stood at their pieces with smiling but tense faces. The American squadron pressed on rapidly in a line as straight as a fleet of boats in tow. A signal from the flagship said, " Fire as convenient," but they all reserved their fire for closer range. When the range-finder showed two miles, Dewey said in a quiet voice to the captain of his ship, the historic words:

" When you are ready, you may fire, Mr. Gridley."

The message instantly reached the eager men at the eight-inch guns in the forward turret, and at just 5.35 the first projectiles were hurled with a flash and a roar at the fated ships of Spain. Like an echo came the boom of the opening fire from all the other American ships, as they discharged their port batteries. The air was full of shells and smoke, and the water was splashed about our ships with the Spanish shot. To give our gunners a better sight the speed was slowed down.

After all had passed the anchored Spanish fleet, our line swung around and returned over the same course, firing the starboard batteries. Suddenly, about a thousand yards ahead of the Olympia, a waterspout arose; a submarine mine had been exploded, but with inaccurate calculation.

When the Spanish flagship, the Reina Cristina, saw that the mine had failed, she slipped her mooring and charged direct at the Olympia, like a maddened pan-

The Battle of Manila Bay, May 1, 1898.

ther. But the guns of all the fleet were upon her, and the marksmanship of the cool-headed American gunners did not fail. No vessel could stand under that gunnery. In a few moments the white ship was·in flames, with great holes torn in her sides, and she turned to flee. But even as she headed to seek safety, the trained eye of a gunner in the Olympia's forward turret sent a terrible projectile after her, which struck her stern and plunged clear through her bow, sweeping down her captain and sixty men. Then it was " save who can."

Admiral Montojo had his boat lowered from the wrecked ship and changed his flag to the Isla de Cuba. This vessel immediately became the target of the resistless American batteries, and soon in her turn she was burning and going down. But before she sank the Admiral signaled to his two torpedo boats to go out and do for the Olympia what he had been unable to accomplish.

Across the bay came charging these little demons of war. The Olympia's big guns first greeted them, but missed their mark, the speed of the boats being so great and the targets so small. They arrived within eight hundred yards and in a moment more would have discharged their torpedoes. But they came no farther. The secondary battery and the rapid-fire guns were now raining their shells and solid shot upon them. From one of them there arose a white explosion, and she dropped under the waves forever. The other, sorely wounded, and dazed by the fate of her consort, turned like the flagship and sought the beach, where she was found later, pierced, shattered, and bloody.

Having once more passed the enemy, our vessels turned around again and steamed back to fire upon the other side. This time it was the Don Antonio de Ulloa and the Castillo that were overwhelmed. Our gunners were worn, but they seemed to gain in precision and fired with the coolness of target practice. The wonderful victory they were gaining lifted them above exhaustion. The Spanish captains had nailed their flags to the masts, and their men were fighting with the desperate bravery of those for whom there is nothing but death.

Then the Olympia drew out of the line, to the surprise of the whole fleet. Some feared that she was in distress, but as she came within hearing of the other ships their men cheered and her men cheered back with such spirit that no further assurance of her condition was needed. Commodore Dewey signaled the fleet to withdraw and serve breakfast.

It was now half-past seven o'clock and the battle had raged more than two hours. Several Spanish vessels were burning and there was also a fire at the arsenal. Yet their guns were still at work with no sign of surrender. Our men were displeased at the order to cease firing and to eat, because the victory had not yet been completely won. They wanted no refreshment while there was a Spanish warship afloat. But the Commodore knew best. He desired to know the condition of his ships and the state of the ammunition. The captains were summoned to the flagship, and soon returned to their vessels with the good news that not a man had been killed in the fleet, and only half a dozen slightly wounded; and they also gave the assurance that the assault would soon be renewed and the battle fought to a finish.

So the fleet drew off to the middle of the bay and waited while the men took breath and had their breakfast; the guns grew cool, the ammunition was reinforced, the machinery was examined, and everything put in fresh order for a finishing onset.

At twenty minutes before eleven the signal came to recommence the attack. The plan of battle had been changed. The Spanish ships had been so much damaged as to be practically out of the fight. Now, instead of the American fleet moving up and down in front of the forts and the Spanish ships, and firing as they went, the orders were to go directly towards them, stop, get the range, then choose a mark and hit it with accuracy. The Baltimore went in first, at full speed, almost disappearing in her own smoke. She not only used her larger guns, but approached so close that she could use the rapid-fire guns in her smaller battery. In twenty minutes the Olympia followed her. Then in turn the Boston, the Raleigh, and the Concord followed. The little Petrel, which drew less water than the rest, ran in and out firing incessantly at the ships and the forts until the sailors named her the " baby battleship." By one o'clock all the larger Spanish vessels were sunk or on fire, and out of action, and the forts were disabled and burning.

Five minutes later the " baby battleship " signaled to the Commodore that the enemy had struck his colors and that a white flag was flying over the fort at Cavite. The battle had now been completely won. The firing ceased and the crews climbed the rigging to cheer and cheer again at the marvelous, triumphant battle seven thousand miles from any American soil. To them it brought enduring fame, and to the officers it brought the thanks of their countrymen and promotion. For a time all rules were suspended; if it should be said that the captains danced with old jack-tars, and the Commodore gave vent to his feelings by hugging the cabin-boy, we could readily believe it.

There had been many false rumors through the fleet about the killed and wounded upon the different vessels. When it was announced that there were none killed and but half a dozen slightly wounded, it seemed impossible. For four hours they had been under the incessant fire of heavy guns. The Olympia had been hit thirteen times, and none of the others had escaped. The intensity of feeling, when it was known that the crews were all safe, made many of the strongest men burst into tears of joy.

It was a battle in which scientific skill had decided the result. The Spaniards had apparently poured their metal into the bay at random. The American commander had maneuvered his fleet with a calm and trained judgment which minimized the effect of the enemy's shots, and the American gunners had used their guns with as much deliberation and precision as though engaged in target practice. It was the triumph of skill and accurate marksmanship over mere daring without training, the victory of manly courage working through science over desperate valor without scientific direction.

The world heard the news of this extraordinary battle with absolute amazement. No battle like it had ever been fought. Destruction as great had befallen the vanquished in other battles, but never before had such annihilation been wrought without the cost of a single life to the victors. Europe instantly comprehended that the United States, notwithstanding the comparative smallness of her navy, was one of the most formidable naval powers in the world. The people in America were in a tumult of joy and pride. While victory had been expected, none could have fancied it to be so complete. It was the most wonderful triumph of American arms in our history. Commodore Dewey, with his officers and men, received the thanks of the President and Congress; he was named Acting Admiral, and soon after was made Rear-Admiral. If the war lacked any popularity before, it was wanting no longer. It was a victory with deeper results in the United States than in Manila.

Following the battle the Petrel steamed out from behind the forts at Cavite with a half-dozen captured vessels in her tow. One of these, the Manila, had six hundred tons of coal and many beef-cattle on board, both of which were needed.   On the next day a detail was sent on shore to bury the Spanish dead and relieve their wounded.   Occasion was taken to advise the Captain-General of the Philippines and the people of Manila that if one shot was fired at the fleet from the fortifications at Manila the city would be laid in ashes. In a day or two the forts at the mouth of the bay were reduced.

Then the fleet settled down to wait nearly three months for an American army to come from over the seas to occupy the city.

CHAPTER VI

The Attack on Santiago

GUANTANAMO, Daiquiri, Guasimas, El Caney, San Juan, and Santiago,—these names mark the landing of the American army in Cuba, and the route of progress to a splendid triumph of American arms on that island. But they stand for much more, —for heroism and aggressiveness, for patience, endurance, and persistence, for hardship and death, for the expulsion of the Spaniard, and the final termination of Spanish rule in America.

The first armed movement towards the expulsion from Cuba of the Spanish army of nearly 200,000 men, was to establish a blockade of naval vessels along the coast in order to cut off from that army all information and supplies.

War actually began on the 21st of April, when the telegraph operator at the White House sent out the President's order to the waiting fleet at Key West to sail instantly to Cuba. For days these warships under Rear-Admiral Sampson had been awaiting that order, ready like racers to spring at the signal. The captains were in the Admiral's cabin on board the New York late in the evening of the 21st when the dispatch arrived. Within an hour the search-lights had begun feeling their way out of the harbor, and before daylight of the 22nd the whole fleet was in the open sea sweeping towards Havana.

There was, as yet, however, no army for invasion. The President had not even called for volunteers when our sailors arrived before Morro Castle. Until an adequate invading force could be gathered and equipped it would have been useless to attempt to batter down the powerful fortifications of Havana. While the new troops were assembling in their various camps, it was the navy's business only to look out for the enemy's fleet, and to isolate the enemy's army from supplies and communication.

Reinforced from day to day with the newly obtained vessels of all sorts, the American Admiral stretched a cordon of blockaders well around the island. The first action of the war was the bombardment of the fortifications of Matanzas, not far eastward from Havana, on the 28th of April. At Cardenas Bay, on the 11th of May, there was a sharp engagement with Spanish batteries and gunboats, in which Ensign Bagley and four men on the torpedo boat Winslow were killed. On the same day several men from the Marblehead were killed while cutting a cable at Cienfuegos. The Spanish Admiral, Cervera, with a formidable fleet, had sailed from Spain, and Sampson cruised eastward to San Juan, Puerto Rico, in the hope of meeting him. Failing to find the Spanish fleet, he bombarded the forts of San Juan for a few hours on the 12th of May, and then returned to Cuba.

A Bird's-Eye View of Santiago and Vicinity.

But meanwhile our new army of over 250,000 men was being mobilized as rapidly as possible. To the impatient people the mustering in, the equipping, and the drilling of these troops seemed to be very slow, and we were shown for the first time how impossible it would have been to meet on even terms an invading army of a first-class European power, like Great Britain, if promptly thrown upon our territory.

From State camps the regiments were transferred to national rendezvous, the most famous of which were Camp Thomas at Chattanooga and Camp Alger near Washington. Thence, as the troops became ready for service, they could be transported to the ports most convenient for embarkation. Tampa, on the west coast of Florida,—the same Tampa where, nearly four centuries before, the Spanish cavalier, De Soto, started on his adventurous march through the unknown lands which now are part of the United States,—was selected as the best point of departure for the expedition to Cuba.

The Fifth Army Corps was encamped here under Major-General Wm. R. Shafter. This body of troops, most of whom were regulars, had the honor of constituting the first expedition of land forces for the rescue of Cuba.

There were several reasons, however, why it seemed wise to delay the expedition. A fleet of transport ships conveying an army over hostile waters is at the mercy of even a very inferior enemy. A single well-directed shell or torpedo could sink a ship carrying a thousand defenseless soldiers. Although the warships which would convoy a fleet of transports might quickly annihilate the enemy's squadron, nevertheless the chance of sinking a number of our crowded transports would warrant any Spanish commander in making the desperate attack. Consequently it would seem like a tempting of fate for a vast expedition of soldiers to venture out until the sea was reasonably safe from the enemy's cruisers and torpedo boats.

Spain proved formidable in her power of sending out misleading rumors. Such contradictory reports were received from various quarters of Europe, as well as from numbers of ports in the neighborhood of the West Indies, that it became impossible to tell where the powerful fleets of Admiral Cervera and Admiral Camara were to be found. They might be in the ports of Spain; they might be at the Canary or Cape Verde Islands; they might be hovering near the New England coast; they might be dodging among the islands of the Caribbean Sea. Certainly, until they were either located or destroyed, the open sea was no place for 16,000 soldiers gathered on the frail transports.

Consequently, from week to week the impetuous army waited on the burning sand at Tampa while the navy seemed to have all the opportunities for service.

The first attempt of the American army to land on the shore of Cuba was made on the 12th of May by the officers and men of the First United States Infantry, who had been sent on the steamer Gussie to carry supplies to the Cubans. The Spaniards, however, had intercepted the Cuban party, and appeared in such force and resisted the attempts to land with such spirit that the Americans withdrew without making connection with their Cuban allies. Though our troops suffered no loss, but inflicted considerable damage upon the Spanish, we were obliged to admit that the first advantage rested with the enemy.

During the next fortnight the fleet of Admiral Cervera arrived on this side of the ocean and was finally discovered in Santiago harbor. The voyage of this hostile force from Cadiz to Santiago was romantic with interest to the world.

When the war broke out, this fleet was at the Cape Verde Islands. These islands belong to Portugal. Our Government protested against the fleet being harbored in a neutral port, in violation of international law. After much delay Portugal informed the Government at Washington, the 26th of April, that the Spanish ships would be given forty-eight hours in which to leave the Cape Verde Islands. On the 28th of April, however, they were still there. But Portugal now definitely declared her neutrality, and Cervera, having had ample time to provision and coal his fleet, steamed leisurely away. Where he had gone was a mystery. He was reported to be at the Canary Islands. He was reported to have arrived in Spain. He was said to have been seen crossing the Atlantic. His fleet, though not large in number, was powerful because of its homogeneity. It had no slow transports to retard its progress. It consisted of the five armored cruisers, the Cristobal Colon, the Infanta Maria Teresa, the Almirante Oquendo, the Vizcaya, the Reina Mercedes, and three swift torpedo-boat destroyers.

A fleet like this, properly officered and worked, could be used like a single machine. Its power of damage to the United States was enormous. It might appear suddenly off Boston harbor and lay that wealthy and poorly defended city in ashes if it refused the tribute of millions which would naturally be demanded. Or it might appear before New York and, though in the face of greater danger to itself, might still inflict inconceivable disaster; again, it might proceed more to the southward and intercept our battleship, the Oregon, then steaming northward on its long voyage from Puget Sound around Cape Horn. It might throw itself into the harbor of San Juan, Puerto Rico, and use that haven as a basis for mischievous operations against the Americans.

From each of these quarters came reports of strange warships having been seen, and our commanders continued, in painful uncertainty, the necessary policy of waiting.

Finally the uncertainty lifted. About the 11th of May the Spanish flotilla was definitely reported at the French island of Martinique, and shortly after, at the island of Curaçao, just north of Venezuela.

While Sampson was returning from his hunt for Cervera at Puerto Rico, the Spaniard was sailing due northwest for Santiago de Cuba, which he reached on the 19th of May. His arrival at Santiago was not

known by the Americans with certainty for several
days. While Sampson kept guard near Key West,
Commodore Schley with the " flying squadron " was
watching the harbor of Cienfuegos on the southern
coast of Cuba, where Cervera was reported to be hidden. At last his hiding-place at Santiago was discovered, and on the 28th of May, Schley, with his
flagship the Brooklyn, accompanied by the Massachusetts, the Texas, the Iowa, the Marblehead, the
Minneapolis, the Castine, the torpedo boat Dupont,
and the auxiliary cruiser St. Paul, the coaling ship
Merrimac, and others, arrived off Santiago; and the
next day they were able to look through the narrow neck of the bottle-shaped harbor and to see the
enemy's ships lying safely at anchor behind the frown-
ing fortifications and the network of submarine torpedoes.

To verify fully the assurance that all of the Spanish
vessels were there, Lieutenant Victor Blue, of the navy,
made a daring and famous reconnoissance. He landed
and, at the greatest risk, climbed the hills, counted
one by one the enemy's ships, and returned with the
report that the five cruisers and two torpedo boats
were actually imprisoned in the bay.

In a few days Rear-Admiral Sampson, with the flagship New York and the battleship Oregon, the cruiser
New Orleans, and several auxiliary vessels and torpedo
boats, reinforced Commodore Schley and took command of the fleet that was keeping Cervera " bottled "
in Santiago.

Then in a few days followed an exploit which awoke the admiration of the world and lifted a hitherto obscure young officer to the summit of fame. Lieutenant Hobson took the coaling ship Merrimac by night beneath the guns of the forts, and while under the most terrible fire from both shores, endeavored to anchor his ship in the narrow channel, to sink her by his own hand, in order thus to leave her wreck to block the Spanish ships if they should attempt to escape. That the Merrimac was not sunk at the precise spot intended was due to the rudder being shot away.

When morning came he and his six companions who had volunteered for the enterprise were, as by a miracle, alive and unhurt, clinging to a raft. The story of that unrivaled exploit is fully told in a later chapter. The fact that the attempt to close the harbor was not fully successful does not detract from the sublime heroism of the men.

The situation now was this: The Spanish fleet was indeed besieged; it might dash for liberty, but, in the face of such a superior and vigilant force, it would have but little chance. On the other hand, the besiegers were unable to reach it so long as it chose to remain in its haven; the narrow channel was a network of submarine mines which would sink the first vessel that entered; and the lofty forts on the cliffs above could at such close range pour down an annihilating torrent of shells upon the thin decks of the attacking ships, which, at that nearness, could not lift their guns sufficiently to silence the batteries. Their elevation was so great that successive bombardments, though they damaged, did not destroy the batteries.

Nevertheless, until they were destroyed or captured it was evident that the ships could not advance into the channel to clear it of its sunken torpedoes. The aid of the army was therefore necessary. A force by land was required to capture the harbor forts, so that the battleships might countermine the channel, steam in, and engage the Spanish fleet.

Accordingly, General Shafter was ordered to take his troops, land near Santiago, and capture the forts.

Before he started, however, the navy, on the 10th of June, made a landing. It was the first permanent foothold gained by Americans on Cuba. Under the protection of the guns of the Oregon, the Marblehead, and the Yosemite, six hundred marines landed at Guantanamo Bay, in command of Lieutenant-Colonel R. W. Huntington. Their landing was stoutly resisted by the Spaniards. All day and all night the fighting continued, as the little band desperately defended their camp from the continuous and encircling volleys. Here were the first American lives lost on Cuban soil. But, in spite of their severe losses, the marines held the flag where they had planted it.

General Shafter's expedition started on the 14th of June. Thirty-five transports carried sixteen thousand men. They went under the protection of fourteen armed vessels of the navy. The battleship Indiana led the way. Six days later they came in sight of Morro Castle at the entrance to the bay of Santiago, and directly they heard the cheers of the crews of the battleships on duty there.

Very soon Rear-Admiral Sampson came aboard to confer with General Shafter, and then both were rowed ashore at Acerraderos, under the protection of the fleet, to confer with the Cuban General, Garcia, and arrange for the landing of the army. As the boat neared the shore the Cuban soldiers plunged into the water and surrounded it, welcoming and cheering the American officers.

On the second morning thereafter, the battleships shelled the shore at four different points along the forty miles of coast in order to mislead the Spaniards; and then at nine o'clock the signal was given for all the troops to go ashore as quickly as possible at Daiquiri, sixteen miles east of the entrance to Santiago harbor and twenty-four miles west of Guantanamo, where the marines were still maintaining the flag they had planted.

In a moment the water was covered with small boats. Men jumped overboard and swam to shore in their anxiety to be first upon the land. Soon the beach was black with American soldiers. The Spaniards had fled in haste, leaving their camp equipment, and in some cases their breakfasts, behind them. Then the unloading of the transports began. Men with little or no clothing upon them went back and forth from the ships to the shore carrying the arms and supplies. The artillery was landed at the one little dock of an iron company. The horses and mules were pushed

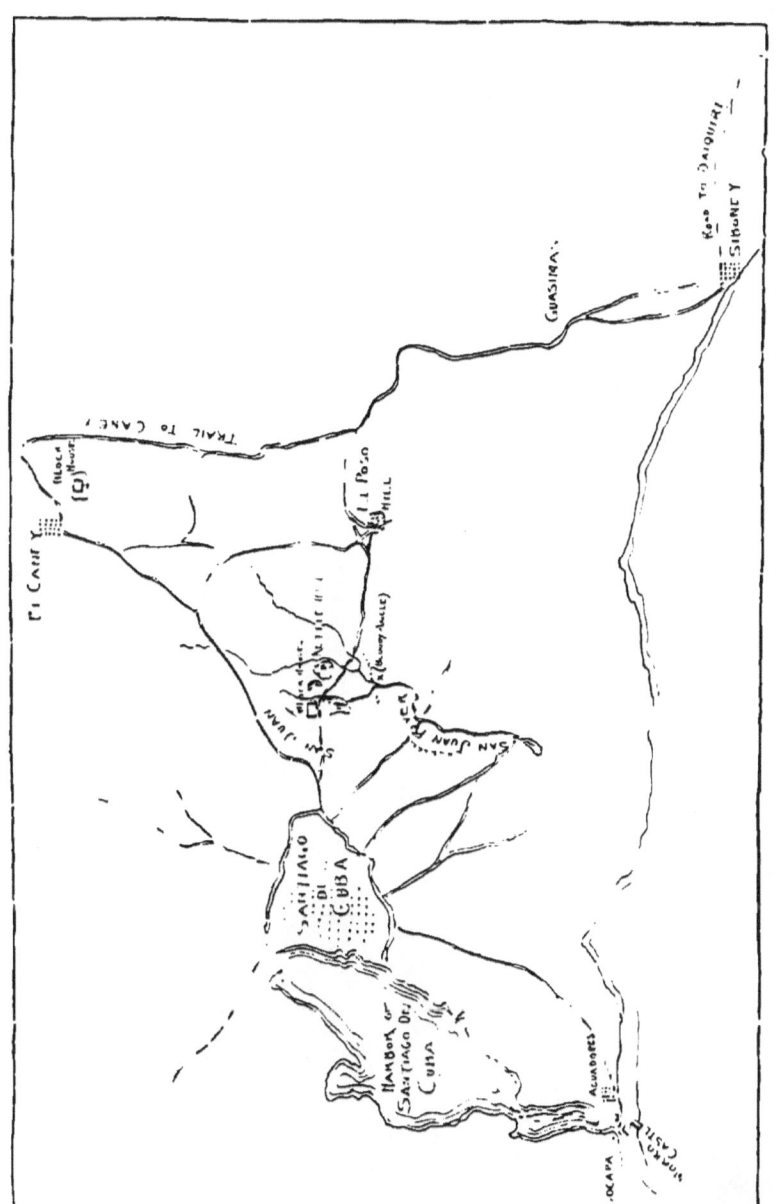

A War-Map of the Santiago Campaign.

overboard and left to swim ashore; though some
of them swam out to the open ocean and forgot to
come back.

In a short time four men were seen climbing the
mountain side hundreds of feet above the level of the
sea. Soon the tiny figures were attracting the attention of the crowd. They were making for the blockhouse at the highest peak. They could be seen to
stop and look into the fort for a moment; then to reach
the house. Directly "Old Glory" appeared waving
against the sky. In an instant every steam whistle in
the great fleet, for miles around, was shrieking, and
every man on the decks and in the rigging of the ships,
in the water and on the shore, was shouting for the
flag of freedom and for what it represented and proclaimed.

The little army was stretched out upon the shore,
and that night its camp-fires sparkled for miles against
the black background of the hills.

The advance upon Santiago was begun immediately.
General Shafter understood clearly that he had more
to fear from climatic sickness than from the enemy's
bullets, and determined to finish the fight with the
greatest rapidity possible. Consequently he did not
wait for the unloading of all his supplies, but pushed
his men forward over the mountain paths with only
such outfit as they could carry on their backs, intending to follow them closely with the heavy artillery and
the baggage-trains.

But he was not aware of the true condition of the

roads.   There were no roads.   What were called such
on the maps were at best but bridle-paths, and more
often mere mountain trails.   These trails passed over
rocks, fallen timber, through swamps, and over bridge-
less streams.   The soldiers, as soon as they began to
march, found themselves an army of mountain climbers.
The sun burned in the breathless glades like a furnace.
It was the rainy season, and each day showers of icy
coldness would pour down for hours; and when the
rain ceased the sun would beat down more fiercely
than before, while the humidity was insupportable.
Sun-baked paths suddenly became mountain torrents;
at one hour the men were suffocated with the fine
dust, the next hour they were wading in mud above
their gaiters.   Strange and unheard-of insects buzzed
about them, and they were followed by an army of
disagreeable attendants with which they soon became
very familiar—clattering land-crabs, the scavengers of
the country.

The progress of the troops was a crawling rather than
a march.   Under the excessive heat thousands of the
soldiers threw away blankets, ponchos, haversacks,
coats, and even underclothing.   The bumping cans of
preserved meat which they carried were cast into the
bush, and many preferred to trust to luck for their
next meal rather than be burdened with even the sim-
plest food.   But guns and cartridge-belts no one threw
away.

Then at night the cool of the evening was quickly
succeeded by a chill which penetrated the wet clothing

Spirit under Difficulties   Boundless Courage

and to the very bone. Yet there was less grumbling
among these soldierly men than would be heard at a
picnic spoiled by a shower. They had one desire, and
that was to get over the ground and reach the enemy.

The Spaniards withdrew as our soldiers advanced.
Most of our men had never heard a gun fired in battle,
but they expected the conflict now to begin at any
time. There was, however, no trepidation; they made
little noise lest they might not get near to the enemy;
they thought how much more fortunate they were
than their fellows in the home camps, because to
them had been given the perilous duty of making the
attack.

CHAPTER VII

The Attack on Santiago

(Continued)

Guasimas

BUT if the army moved slowly, events moved rapidly. On the second day, even before the whole army was ashore, the first battle with loss of life occurred. The troops were advancing by different paths to take position on the line of battle which was to surround the city. Near the center was the First Regiment of United States Volunteer Cavalry, popularly called the " Rough Riders."

This regiment of cowboys and ranchmen, with a sprinkling of college men and young fellows of wealth and social position, was commanded by Colonel Leonard Wood and Lieut.-Colonel Theodore Roosevelt. The former had been a surgeon in the regular army with military training in Western campaigns on the plains. The latter was one of the best known young men in the Republic; famous for his courageous honesty in politics and for his patriotic energy in civil administration. He had resigned the position of Assistant Secretary of the Navy to organize this

unique regiment under the command of his friend
Colonel Wood.

The Rough Riders had left their horses in Florida
because of the difficulty of transportation and the lack
of open ground in Cuba. As they were threading
their way on foot over the hills, their trail joined that
of the regulars at the place called Guasimas. There
they received a sudden volley from the enemy concealed in the thick glades, but they held their ground
and returned the fire. They were unable to see their
foes, whose smokeless powder gave no trace of their
location; but through the tall grass and brush they
steadily pushed on in the face of the dropping death,
firing with calm precision. One after another of the
Riders dropped dead or grievously wounded, but these
young men, who had never been under fire, no more
thought of turning back than a college team at a football game. Their colonels handled carbines like the
men and were at every point in the line which they
had deployed through the brush.

Soon they were joined by the colored regulars, and
then they fought on together. Between the Rough
Riders and the regulars engaged there were about one
thousand men, and they were fighting four thousand
Spaniards.

The wounded that could walk were urged to go to
the rear, but most of them refused; and, sitting at the
foot of the trees, continued their deadly marksmanship at any sign of the Spanish. When there was an
opening in the glades the men crouched and crawled

6

toward the enemy; when there was a little protection
of trees, they dashed forward, firing as they went.
The Spaniards did not understand this kind of fighting.   According to *their* rules, after such murderous
volleys as they had poured into the Americans, their
enemy should have fallen back.   Instead of this, as
one of the Spanish prisoners said: " They kept push-
ing forward as if they were going to take us with their
hands."

After two hours of this fighting, under the unfalter-
ing advance and accurate fire of the Americans, the
Spanish volleys became less frequent and effective.
Then the Spaniards broke and ran.   When the battle
was over, the American soldiers had lost sixteen killed
and fifty-two wounded, but they were two miles nearer
Santiago than when they met their first fire.

It had been a strange battle, and one that appealed
peculiarly to the patriotic pride of the American people.   On that day, college men and the bronzed men
of the plains, millionaires and negroes, all were standing upon the common level of American citizenship,
true brothers in devotion to duty; and there were no
differences in courage or manliness.

El Caney

The Spaniards seemed to have a curious notion of
the Americans as fighters; they thought that after a
sharp resistance they would draw back, and that on the
next morning they would be gone.   Instead, the

Americans were nearer to Santiago on each succeeding day of their exhausting climbing. Slowly and surely the lines drew up around the city. The Spanish garrison numbered some thirteen thousand men, amply supplied with ammunition, behind trenches and barbed-wire fences which were so well arranged as to excite the admiration of our engineers.

The country around was filled with Spanish soldiers. Everyone knew that the heaviest work was yet to be done. The American troops, however, had a more dreaded enemy than the Spaniards. The intolerable heat, the soaking rains, the piercing night chills, the lack of proper food, and, above all, the miasma of the ground were daily preying upon the vitality of the soldiers who had come so robust and hardy from their American camps.

It was feared that an epidemic of yellow fever or typhoid fever was at hand. It certainly was. What was to be done must evidently be done quickly. Moreover, the whole army had a natural ambition to see the Stars and Stripes floating over Santiago by the Fourth of July.

Around and above Santiago was an open plateau. Here the dense and tangled thickets and the mountain trails ended. The problem before General Shafter was to close around Santiago and capture it before General Linares with his thirteen thousand soldiers could escape, and before General Pando, marching from the north, could throw in his reinforcement of eight thousand men.

The city of Santiago is so located, at the head of its long harbor, that a complete line of investiture would stretch from the seacoast on the east to a point near the head of the harbor on the west of the city—a line which resembled a huge fishhook. At the northern end of this line, where the shank of the hook begins to turn into the curve, and about four miles northeast from Santiago, is the suburb of El Caney; one mile east is San Juan.

The hills of El Caney and San Juan each slope rather sharply to the eastward, the direction from which our troops were coming. Between the foot of these ridges and the woods is open country. To march across this open is difficult because of gulleys, winding streams, thick grass, and low bush.

The suburb of El Caney nestles on the hillsides, and here the rich Santiagoans had built country residences. On the top of San Juan were farmhouses. The Spanish engineers had perceived how ugly these bluffs might be made to an invading army, and had transformed the farmhouses and country seats into forts, with ramparts of broken stone and bags of sand, and with loopholes made in the walls.

Each hill was also crowned by a blockhouse fort. Indeed, a score of these little forts, which had previously proved so effectual against the Indian-like attacks of the Cubans, stretched along the commanding ridges outside of Santiago.

In addition, on the face of the eastern ridge there were admirably constructed lines of rifle-pits, and below these were interminable barbed-wire fences, which were the clever invention of General Weyler for retarding any daring enemy who might have the temerity to charge across the deadly open and up the hills.

If the reader has been able to make a mental picture from this brief description he will comprehend the grave problem before the American generals. In the lines on lines of trenches and inside the little forts were desperate defenders, with terrible rapid-firing Mauser rifles, which, if scientifically used, might sweep from the earth any body of troops advancing across the mile or more of clear country. In view of this kind of advantage, common military prudence would seem to dictate that no charge be made against these defenses until they had been pulverized by artillery.

But, on the other hand, because of the impossible roads, General Shafter could not bring up his siege-guns; indeed, these powerful pieces were never landed from the transports. It had taken days to get even the light batteries of Captains Capron and Grimes over the dozen miles from the landing-place to a position in front of the bluffs of El Caney and San Juan. General Shafter reasoned that the risk of attacking these positions with infantry only partially supported by artillery was less than the danger of fever under the exhausting conditions of the climate. The result seemed to justify this reasoning.

A general advance along the whole length of the American line was begun in the afternoon of the 30th of June. General Lawton's division was to attack El

Caney.   General Kent's division, with General Wheeler's division of dismounted cavalry, was to move against San Juan.   General Duffield's brigade was to proceed against Aguadores, which was on the seacoast south of San Juan and a little east of Morro Castle.

With General Lawton, for the attack on El Caney, was Captain Capron's battery; and for the attack on San Juan, Captain Grimes's battery had been assigned. On the morning of the 1st of July, General Lawton's division was in the shape of a half-circle around El Caney.   At five o'clock in the morning the advance on the town was commenced.   It was said by some that there would be little resistance and that the town would be taken before breakfast.   As the troops got nearer to the enemy's trenches the knowing ones enjoined silence lest the Spaniards should hear them and run away.   Before the day was out there were many times when these same knowing ones wished that the Spaniards would run away.

Before the sun had appeared above the high mountain peaks behind them, the cannoneers had taken their places and trained their four pieces on the stone fort which was perched on the apex of the hill of El Caney.   At sunrise the Spanish flag was run up its staff, and immediately the American guns opened fire. At first our shells brought no answer, but soon the Spanish artillery began to drop their shells into our lines with an unexpected accuracy, while from the trenches and the loopholes of the stone fort and of the fortified houses the infantry poured at our position a sweeping and effective fire. The rifle bullets seemed to come in sheets, like horizontal rain; and upon our soldiers lying on the ground the grass-tops clipped by the bullets fell like leaves.

But from the American lines the incessant stream of Krag-Jörgensen bullets, as well as the artillery, was doing terrible destruction. The Spaniards had the better position and stronger defenses; but the Americans had the coolness and a vastly superior accuracy of aim. Our soldiers fired as deliberately as at a marksmanship contest; wherever a Spanish straw hat was seen above the trenches, or an officer exposed himself, there was a target for a dozen rifles; before that scientific aiming each loophole in the blockhouse became a point of fatal exposure.

But instead of ending before breakfast the battle lasted all day. Our men were dying on every side. One journalist who was with the command counted twenty-five dead in an hour. The officers advised and steadied the men, who were no less heroic than themselves; yet many officers disdained to crouch as they compelled their men to do, and, as conspicuous targets, were dropping in large numbers.

For most of these soldiers it was their first battle; yet there was no evidence of panic, nor was there a single act of cowardice observed. The foreign military attachés who were present were astounded at the steadiness of these soldiers, who were receiving their first baptism of fire. Among the wounded there was no complaint at the necessary delay of attention; under the broiling sun they waited patiently and almost without a groan until they could be removed.

All the morning and long into the afternoon the creeping advance continued. The smokeless powder of the Spaniards often made their fire bewildering. The storm of bullets came from new directions, and when it was discovered that the bodies of the men were being hit on a different side, the masked batteries and trenches had to be first coolly located and then silenced.

The Spanish sharpshooters penetrated between our regiments, hid themselves among the trees, and fired upon the wounded as they were staggering to the rear. When this was discovered our men were beside themselves with rage. But the regulars only moved forward a few feet farther and aimed their Krag-Jörgensens with more dogged determination.

Thus, until the middle of the afternoon, the very slow advance went on; the dark blue shirts writhed forward from bush to bush, and yard by yard shortened the distance; sometimes little dashes were made from one poor protection to another, but every one of these short rushes was a deadly adventure. It was a battle under new conditions. The long distance and rapid fire of the new rifle would have annihilated one of those old-fashioned line-of-battle charges which were made in the Civil War.

Finally, at half-past three, the town which was to have been taken before breakfast seemed to be as bristling and unsubdued as ever. The time had at last come for a desperate charge. The broken and bushy

The Charge at El Caney, July 1, 1898.

ground had been crossed, and our men were facing the very trenches. The order was passed down the line for a general rush. With a roaring cheer the regiments leaped to their feet and dashed at the hill. They did not go in ranks—scarcely in companies. It was a race to reach the trenches and to swarm around the fort.

Captain Haskell, of the Twelfth Infantry, was conspicuous in the rush; his long white beard streaming back like the plume of Henry of Navarre. Officers and men dropped down in appalling numbers in the gusts of death. But no force was able to check that charge. Prying down the barbed-wire fences, cheering with that thunderous yell which only Americans can give, they closed over the trenches, which were found filled with dead men. In a moment more the blue uniforms were seen around the fortifications on the hilltop; the barricaded doors were broken in and holes were made in the roofs.

But the Spaniards had finished their fight. The barricaded streets of El Caney offered little resistance. A few shots more, and the town was in the hands of the exhausted but jubilant Americans.

Superb in this charge were the colored soldiers of the Twenty-fourth Regiment. At Guasimas colored troops had saved the Rough Riders; at El Caney they fought with no less heroism. The officers of our regular army say that no better soldiers ever wore a uniform, and prisoners taken from the fort at El Caney insisted that the colored troops were nine feet tall and could strangle them with their fists.

At half-past four the American troops had possession of the town. They found the Spanish dead lying in lines in the blockhouse behind the loopholes from which they had fired. The dead were in the streets and in the houses. The trenches were open graves. When the little fort was broken into, only one Spanish officer and four men were alive out of the entire garrison.

The forces on the opposing sides had been about equal. Had the Spaniards been as skillful with their arms as the Americans, the result might have been longer delayed, and perhaps there might have been another result altogether. But the Spanish were proud and daring men, and they made the most stubborn resistance that Americans have ever met from a foreign foe.

If the Americans appreciated the dogged courage of the Spaniards, the enemy was amazed at the invincible gallantry of the invaders. One of the surviving Spanish officers has told the story of the battle, and in it he said:

" The enemy's fire was incessant, and we answered with equal rapidity. I have never seen anything to equal the courage and dash of those Americans, who, stripped to the waist, offering their naked breasts to our murderous fire, literally threw themselves on our trenches, on the very muzzles of our guns.

" Our execution must have been terrible. We had the advantage of our position and mowed them down by hundreds, but they never retreated or fell back an inch. As one man fell, shot through the heart, another would take his place with grim determination and unflinching devotion to duty in every line of his face.

"Their gallantry was heroic. We wondered at these men, who fought like lions and fell like men courting a wholesale massacre, which could well have been avoided had they only kept up their firing without storming our trenches."

The number of Spanish dead is unknown. But three hundred and seventy-seven American soldiers were killed and wounded. They were martyrs in the cause of humanity; they fell, not for the mere purpose of capturing an insignificant Spanish village, but to make a people who were their neighbors free.

After taking El Caney the American outposts were at once pushed forward beyond the town and also within rifle-shot of the intrenchments of San Juan.

San Juan

While the battle of El Caney was going on, the troops there engaged could hear the roar of the guns of El Poso, which had opened on San Juan on their left, about three miles south.

El Poso is a hill about a mile and a half from the hill of San Juan. The plan of the commander-in-chief was that General Lawton, who took El Caney on the 1st of July, should finish that work early in the morning; that then his troops should push south to San

Juan, join with the troops of Generals Sumner and
Kent, and spend the night in front of San Juan. The
next morning the entire force was to attack San Juan
on both sides.

This plan was never carried out. General Lawton
did not finish capturing El Caney until the end of the
afternoon. But meantime the American forces in
front of San Juan could not endure being shot to
pieces by the Spaniards, and so went forward to capture San Juan without the aid of the troops from El
Caney.

The hill of San Juan is just outside of the city of
Santiago directly to the east. Looked at on its eastern
side it seems like a sharp bluff. On top of the hill was
a low farmhouse with broad eaves. This had been
turned into a fortification by the Spanish, as had also
a long shed near by. East of this farmhouse, near the
edge of the hill, were long rows of Spanish trenches;
back of the farmhouse, towards Santiago, was a slight
dip in the ground, and on the rise towards the city were
more trenches. Barbed-wire fences were everywhere.

Looking eastward from the bluff of San Juan hill is
a meadow one third of a mile in width, before you get
to the brush and trees of the forest. This meadow, in
the main, is a tangle of high grass, broken by scattered
trees and barbed-wire fences. A little way to the
northeast from San Juan is a shallow duck-pond, and
just beyond this water is a low hill which, from its
great sugar kettles on top, our men called Kettle Hill.
Beyond the rolling meadow are the woods, broken by

swift winding streams; through this timber come the irregular, mountainous trails from Siboney, along which the troops had toiled, and on either side of which they had bivouacked for several days.

General Shafter, from his headquarters two or three miles distant from the edge of the forest, had ordered the troops of the First Division, under General Kent, which was to attack San Juan, to march forward all at once through this narrow trail and form in line of battle as they emerged at the edge of the woods. The road in some places was a hundred feet broad, in others it was not more than ten; practically it was no wider anywhere than at its narrowest part, and as the troops entered the road from their bivouacs there was an almost instant jam. While thus crowded they found themselves under fire without knowing whence the bullets came. It was at last discovered that the tree-tops concealed large numbers of Spanish sharpshooters. Several companies of colored troops were at once ordered into a thicket to bring down these sharpshooters without quarter. After a time the marching crowd was thus partially relieved of its hidden enemies; but the troops, as they neared the edge of the woods, came within the fire of both the Spanish artillery and rifles, and men began to fall rapidly. The confusion of the narrow road was bewildering; two brigades were marching side by side and became hopelessly intermingled. Orders were issued and countermanded; and sometimes the reversal of an order reached an officer before the order itself.

The war balloon, which had been at the head of the troops, had served the Spanish as a fatal index of our location, and was the cause of much of the early slaughter of the day. Before it came down, however, it had discovered a fork in the road to the left, which led to the open meadow. Through this fork a portion of the troops was at once hurried.

But the Spaniards well knew the points where the two roads emerged into the open meadow, and those spots were pens of death.

Thus the morning hours wore on, seemingly without end. From the high hill of El Poso, Captain Grimes's battery began firing early in the morning at the trenches and the fortified farmhouse. But its old-fashioned powder enveloped it in smoke after each discharge, and it was at least a minute before a second aim could be taken, while its cloud of smoke made it a conspicuous target for the Spaniards; therefore it soon ceased firing and took a new position nearer the enemy.

There was a steady march of wounded men towards the rear; motionless dead were everywhere. Fainting under the heat of the sun and in the suffocation of the tall grass on the sides of the road, men were at the extremity of their endurance, with lolling tongues and staring eyes.

At last endurance was no longer possible. There were no general orders to advance, for the brigade commanders knew that they had been ordered into this position, and they had received no orders from headquarters to get out of it.

The Charge without Orders | The Irresistible Rush

Then the colonels and captains took the matter into their own hands. Somehow, about noon a forward movement began. Conspicuous among the leaders were General Hawkins and Colonel Roosevelt. Soldiers fell in behind any officers who would lead. Lieutenant Ord, who fell dead at the top of the hill, shouted as he started, "All who are brave, follow me." Each officer rallied all the men he could reach.

There was little regard for regimental formation, but in groups the heroes plunged forward. They did not run fast, for the grass was too thick and the obstacles too sharp; yet they panted forward through the tall grass, through the morass, and up the steep hill, aiding one another and pulling themselves up by the bushes.

Those who beheld from the hill of El Poso believed the desperate soldiers would be destroyed to a man. That they were not swept out of existence in the face of that torrent of incessant fire seems a miracle. But they reserved their own fire until they were so close to the trenches that they could see the whites of their enemies' eyes, and then they aimed with such accuracy that in a few moments there was not a living Spaniard in the intrenchments.

Then they rushed against the blockhouse; presently that fortification ceased to spit its fire, its garrison was dead, and the Stars and Stripes were waving over its spreading roof.

The Spanish commander-in-chief, General Linares, had fallen wounded, and the few surviving defenders of San Juan were running towards Santiago. It was estimated that seventy per cent. of the Spanish in the trenches and the blockhouse had fallen.

No such battle had American troops ever fought before. The positions they had taken were, from a military point of view, invincible; yet they had taken them almost with bare hands. It was not a battle where strategy had won; generalship had seemed to fall to pieces; it was the unconquerable nerve of the individual soldier which had triumphed.

When the hilltop was carried, and the flag waved over the blockhouse, the afternoon was half gone. Since daylight the troops had been exposed to the most terrible fire ever experienced on this hemisphere. They were fainting under a tropical sun; they were weak from hunger and thirst; they knew that their generals were practically helpless.

Then, when they found that they were left to themselves, because they were Americans they did not stampede to the rear, but made that immortal charge. This was the battle of San Juan.

While the battles of El Caney and San Juan were being fought, on that same 1st of July the Third Division of General Shafter's army was attacking the base of Morro Castle near Aguadores. The fleet was expected to coöperate in this attack. The Spaniards, however, dynamited the long trestle-bridge across which General Duffield's troops were expected to march; and under the sweeping fire of the enemy it proved impossible to make the attack.

When night fell on the 1st of July the American army had won two victories. But the cost had been terrible. Two hundred and thirty men had been killed, and twelve hundred and eighty-four were wounded. Many were missing. In other words, out of the attacking forces at El Caney and San Juan, every sixth man had fallen. The remainder had been strained to the utmost, and their commanders realized that the next worst thing to a crushing defeat was a costly victory.

The next day, when General Shafter gathered in the reports, he was deeply depressed, and considered the advisability of falling back. Other counsels prevailed, however. Officers and men who heard of it resented the suggestion, and the thin line held its own.

All night long, after the battles, the tired men worked industriously in building intrenchments on the other side of San Juan, anticipating that the Spaniards would attempt to retake it. Now and then there was some fighting through the night, but at no time was there any serious danger of losing the ridge.

The next morning the Spaniards began firing at daylight and the battle raged all day with more or less fury. The losses were considerable, and the suffering of the troops was great, but the advantage gained was securely held. The day was occupied by our artillery in securing good positions to shell the city. At ten o'clock the next night a serious attack was made upon the American line with the purpose of breaking through, but it was effectually repulsed. The third

7

day (Sunday) there was some firing, but not with much spirit. On the morning of that day General Shafter demanded the surrender of Santiago. The demand was not complied with, but the American army was content to rest a little, recover from the shock of battle, and gather up its strength.

As a fact, this gallant army was so seriously crippled by its losses as to make the task of taking the city of Santiago, against fortifications and intrenchments, and with a great fleet of Spanish cruisers lying in the bay, an exceedingly difficult and dangerous one,—indeed, almost an impossible one. Our fleet guarding the mouth of the bay was restrained from entering because of the submarine mines with which the bay was filled. There was not a man on the ships who would not have cheered the order to do so, but the Government was unwilling to risk the loss of our battleships.

That was not all. The Government did not want to destroy the Spanish vessels so much as to capture them. The objective point of the campaign was to take Santiago with its garrison, and with it the Spanish fleet. From the beginning the orders had been to capture rather than destroy the fleet. This made the task of the army indeed grave. The most experienced officers say that it would have cost at least five thousand men to force the inner fortifications and take the city. On that fateful Sunday morning, the little army of Americans, with this great work before them, with enemies on every side, two thirds of them mere boys of the college age, did not number ten thousand effective men. The only thing to be done was to keep what they had gained, get rest, and hold on for reinforcements. Their weakened state was of course not known by the enemy, and when they so boldly demanded the surrender of the city, the Spanish were too concerned over their own losses to build hopes on the weakness of the American army.

That Sunday afternoon General Chaffee, riding along the front of his brigade, said to Col. O'Brien and Major Brush of the Seventeenth Infantry: "Gentlemen, we have lost all we came for; the game has flown; the Spanish fleet is forty miles away on the high seas."

CHAPTER VIII

Destruction of Cervera's Fleet

INDEED, that Sunday morning (the 3rd of July, 1898)
was a fateful hour in the history of the world's contest for freedom.   While the army behind the city of
Santiago held the ground they had gained at such cost,
and waited for the next onset knowing how serious it
must be, the battleships and cruisers in Admiral Sampson's squadron were riding at the mouth of Santiago
Bay,—waiting, waiting, and hoping for the moment
when the trying routine of watching would be dropped
for the roar and dash of a great naval engagement.

There was the armored cruiser Brooklyn, capable of
twenty-one knots an hour, with Commodore Schley,
the second officer in the squadron, on board—the same
Schley who years before took out of the Arctic snows
the dying survivors of the Greely Expedition and
brought them home.   There was the first-class battleship Oregon, fresh from her long journey of fifteen
thousand miles from Puget Sound, around Cape Horn,
and her sister ship the Indiana, both with their
eighteen-inch walls of steel and thirteen-inch guns
which throw a projectile five miles.   Every charge in
these guns requires more than five hundred pounds of
powder; every shell weighs more than half a ton; and

every discharge, at the pressure of an electric button, costs five hundred and sixty dollars. There was the battleship Texas, called a " hoodoo " because of her many misfortunes, but now to become famous for her brilliant work. There was also the battleship Iowa with " Fighting Bob " Evans in command. In the neighborhood was the battleship Massachusetts, as well as other cruisers, torpedo boats, and ocean-liners and pleasure yachts converted into ships of war.

The commander of the fleet, Rear-Admiral Sampson, was absent for the first time in many weeks. Under the orders of President McKinley and knowing the extremity in which the army was placed he had steamed a few miles east with the flagship New York to confer with General Shafter, and if possible afford relief. He had repeatedly said, " If I go away something will happen."

This morning was not unlike most of the others during the five weeks of waiting. The sun was hot and the water calm. The ships drifted about in the deep waters and occasionally steamed up to keep their positions. As it was Sunday, at nine o'clock the men were rigged in clean white suits ready for inspection and for religious service. Everyone looked forward to another day of tedious watching.

At about half-past nine, just as the bugle sounded for service upon the Texas, the navigator on the forward bridge of the Brooklyn called out through his megaphone: " After bridge there! Report to the Commodore and the captain that the enemy's ships are coming out.'' At the same instant the boom of a gun on the Iowa attracted attention and a string of little flags up her rigging signaled: '' The enemy's ships are escaping to the westward.''

In an instant, on every vessel, all was commotion where a moment before there had been perfect order. But even the excitement showed absolute system, for with a rush every man in all the crews was in his place for battle, every vessel was moving up, and every gun was ready for action. From the first warning of the lookout to the boom of the guns it was less than three minutes.

The New York was just ready to land Rear-Admiral Sampson at a point seven miles east of Morro Castle. In twenty minutes he would have been riding over the hills to the headquarters of the army. But the leap of the ships was seen and the flagship was instantly put about and started under highest steam for the fray, while all on board wondered at the cruel fate which had made it necessary for her and the commander to be away on that particular morning.

The increasing clouds of black smoke in the bay showed beyond doubt that at last the enemy's fleet had started upon a grand and desperate dash for liberty. Directly, the Spanish flagship, the Maria Teresa, thrust her nose out of the opening and was followed by the other armored cruisers, the Vizcaya, Cristobal Colon, and Almirante Oquendo, and the torpedo-boat destroyers, Pluton and Furor. The vessels were from eight hundred to twelve hundred yards apart and oc-

cupied from twelve to fifteen minutes in passing the cape at the mouth of the harbor. As they did so they turned to the west, most of the American ships being just then a little to the east of the entrance.

As the Spanish cruisers came in range they opened their batteries upon the Americans, but continued to fly to the westward with all the speed they could make. The two torpedo craft made directly for the Brooklyn, intending to score a point in the chase by destroying the American vessel having the greatest speed. As the American ships closed up, the shore batteries on both sides of the opening began a heavy fire upon them.

The guns of the American fleet opened with terrific effect at the first moment of opportunity. The Brooklyn realized in an instant that it was to be a chase and that she was to lead it. She steamed at the Spanish flagship and at the Vizcaya at full speed. She had been a rival of the Vizcaya at Queen Victoria's Jubilee the year before. She turned a complete circle so as to use all of her batteries to advantage. The Iowa and the Texas rained their great shells upon the enemy with fearful effect.

The little converted yacht Gloucester, under Lieutenant Commander Richard Wainwright, a former officer of the Maine, comprehended that it was her business to take care of the torpedo boats, and appeared to imagine that she was a battleship instead of an unprotected pleasure yacht. She ran in at close range, sometimes being completely hidden by smoke, and worked her small, rapid-firing guns accurately and with deadly results.

The Gloucester received orders by signal to get out of danger, but Wainwright said the signal seemed to him to order him to close in. This commander had a terrible score to settle because of the Maine. From the night of her destruction he had been grimly awaiting his opportunity. Now that his chance had come, he fought his little yacht with a fury that bewildered the Spaniards and amazed the American fleet.

He explained that he was afraid he might strain his guns if he used them at long range! so he got as close to the enemy as he could, firing at the big ships as well as the torpedo craft. His fire was so rapid and exact that the enemy were not able even to launch their torpedoes; one torpedo squad after another being swept away before they could load their tubes.

Hardly had the battle opened before one of the largest guns sent a shell through the Pluton which practically broke her in two. The Furor tried to seek refuge behind the cruisers, but the Gloucester ran in and out and riddled her with an unerring fire which reached her vitals and sent her plunging towards the shore, to break upon a reef and go down under the rolling surf. Some of her crew were helped upon the gallant little vessel which had destroyed her. Out of one hundred and forty men on the two vessels but twenty-four survived.

In fifteen minutes the Maria Teresa and the Oquendo were on fire. At a quarter-past ten the former of these was completely disabled, gave up the fight, and ran on the shore at a point about six and a half miles from the harbor, and in another quarter of an hour the other did the same thing a half-mile farther on. One had been hit thirty-three and the other sixty-six times.

The Vizcaya, in three-quarters of an hour more, struck her colors and turned to the shore fifteen miles from the harbor.

These vessels were pierced by our shells in many places; they were burning, and their guns and ammunition bursting, with the likelihood that their magazines would explode at any moment. As the only resort in the last extremity, they were run on the beach, where they sank and careened over on their sides. Hundreds of their crews were dead and wounded and many more jumped into the heavy sea to save themselves.

The American boats went quickly to their rescue. As the Texas passed one of the stranded vessels her men started a cheer, but Captain Philip, with fine chivalry, told them not to cheer when other brave men were dying. The Iowa and the Ericsson took off the crew of the Vizcaya, and the Gloucester and the Harvard those of the Maria Teresa and the Oquendo. Lieutenant-Commander Wainwright received Admiral Cervera at his gangway and made the defeated Spanish officer as comfortable as possible. The men helped the Spaniards from the water and at great risk went aboard their vessels to carry off the wounded. No trouble or danger was too great to stand in the way of giving help and comfort to the men who had been conquered.

In the meantime, while her sister ships were being destroyed, the Cristobal Colon had pushed on out of the thickest of the fire, and was hoping to escape. She was their best and fastest vessel. When the Vizcaya went ashore, fifteen miles from the start, the fleetness of the Colon had put her ahead of the rest about six miles. As soon as the fate of the Vizcaya was assured, the Iowa and the Indiana were directed to return to the blockading station, and the Brooklyn, the Oregon, the Texas, and the Vixen started on the great race for the Colon.

It was a wonderful race. The high speed of the Brooklyn enabled her to lead the way. But the Oregon showed that she had speed as well as great guns. Her chief engineer had for weeks saved some choice Cardiff coal for just such an emergency, and now it was piled upon the fires with signal effect. The grimy heroes under the decks won the race that day. In the boiler-rooms the heat was almost insufferable, ranging from one hundred and twenty to one hundred and fifty degrees, Fahrenheit. The men fainted often and had to be lifted to the deck where the fresh air could revive them. But there was no flinching or complaint. Frequently the stokers insisted upon working overtime. No one of them in the pit was less intense or less a hero than the captain on the bridge. Once, during the chase, when some of the firemen had fainted, the engineer called to the captain, " If my men can hear a few guns they will revive."

The Colon hugged the coast for the purpose of land-

Charge of the Brooklyn and the Oregon in the Sea-Fight of July 3, 1898.

ing if she could not escape. The pursuers struck a line for a projecting headland. There was no firing for a long distance and the crews watched the great race from the decks. The Brooklyn and the Oregon gradually drew away from the others and gained upon the Spaniard. Their smoke almost hid them from view at times, but when in sight the onrushing cruiser and battleship made a spectacle more magnificent than most of us will ever see.

The Colon fired a shot at her pursuers now and then, but each fell wide of the mark. When Commodore Schley was told by the navigator that the distance between the Colon and the Oregon was but eight thousand five hundred yards, or five miles, he signaled to the battleship to try a thirteen-inch shell upon her. Instantly it whistled over the head of the Brooklyn and fell but little short of the Colon. A second one struck beyond her. A few shots were then fired by both of the American vessels. At twenty minutes after one o'clock the Colon struck her colors and ran ashore forty-two miles from the entrance to Santiago harbor. The Spanish crew scuttled and left her sinking. The Brooklyn and the Oregon soon came up and Captain Cook of the former went aboard and received her surrender. Soon the noble vessel sank in deep water, but was pushed upon the beach by the New York, which had arrived. The next day only a small part of the stern of the ship remained above the water.

All the living men upon the stranded fleet, about sixteen hundred of them, were taken prisoners. The

Spanish Admiral and most of the prominent officers were among the number. All were treated with the utmost kindness, and the wounded received every possible aid, far more than they would have had if they had not been captured.

The Spaniards had four hundred killed. The charred remains found upon their burning ships told too plainly how dreadfully they had suffered. The Americans lost but one man. George H. Ellis, a yeoman, assisting on the bridge of the Brooklyn, was asked by Captain Cook to give him the distance to the Vizcaya. He stepped into the open, took the observation, answered, " Twenty-two hundred yards, sir," and fell at the captain's feet, for a shell had taken off his head.

The naval battle at Santiago, even more completely than that at Manila, showed the decisive superiority of scientific training over haphazard methods of warfare. The Spanish vessels and their armament at Santiago were superior to those at Manila, but the hardy, trained men who worked the American ships and the expert gunners who sighted the American guns gave their adversaries no chance in either battle.

The great victory opened the gates of Santiago and saved thousands of lives in the thinned little army which in its three days' fighting had almost gained admission. Aside from the spell it cast upon the world as an unsurpassed and perfect feat of warfare, this sea-fight was understood at once to be a most significant event in the history of the United States and in the progress of republican institutions.

There were but few who were so thoughtless as not to be stirred with the feeling which possessed the heart of Captain Philip and the crew of the battleship Texas when, as they stood on the deck with uncovered heads and reverent souls on the afternoon of the engagement, the knightly old sailor said: " I want to make public acknowledgment here that I believe in God, the Father Almighty.   I want all you officers and men to lift your hats and from your hearts offer silent thanks to the Almighty for the victory he has given us."   That was the spirit which pervaded all the crews.   Captain Evans wrote: " Every drop of blood in my body was giving thanks."

But it was not the mere victory over a foe that caused this general and thoughtful lifting of heart; it was exultation at the triumph of justice and the progress of freedom.

CHAPTER IX

The Winning of Cuba and Puerto Rico

The Surrender of Santiago

THE army did not know until the next day after the occurrence that the Spanish fleet, which their advance had forced out of the harbor, had been utterly destroyed. The momentous news was carried by dispatch boat and telegraph to all parts of the world and was being celebrated throughout the United States, and indeed by Americans in nearly all of the capitals of Europe, before the gallant army upon the hills around Santiago could know about it.

The report received on Sunday that the enemy's fleet had successfully escaped was naturally a hard disappointment to the army of American boys in the wet trenches: one in six of them had been either killed or wounded; many more were already stricken with the dreaded fevers; and for a time it seemed as if with all their sacrifices and victories the chief object of the campaign had been lost. But the following day, the 4th of July, the true story passed along the lines, and the national anniversary was celebrated on the Santiago hills with such cheers and with such loving appreciation of "The Star-Spangled Banner" as these boys had never imagined before.

The destruction of the fleet changed the feeling in the Spanish as well as in the American army. It not only took away a great force which had been relied upon for protection, but made it clear that before many days the American battleships, mines or no mines, would enter the harbor, and that, between the assaulting army and the navy, the garrison and the city would, if necessary, be destroyed together.

In both camps there was now a new meaning to the demand for surrender. On the one side it was no longer made as a pretense to divert the soldiers' thoughts and to hide the crippled condition of the army, but it was pressed with the confidence that it must quickly be complied with; and on the other side it was now faced as inescapable.

The Spanish commander-in-chief, General Linares, was too seriously wounded to remain in command, but the next officer, General Toral, refused to yield to the demand for surrender. The truce, however, was maintained, at the earnest request of the foreign consuls in the city, in order to give the women and children time to escape before the assault should be renewed.

In the meantime the parleying about the surrender was continued, and the general officers of both armies held meetings under a tree between the lines. On our side there was a strong desire to avoid further bloodshed, and this desire seemed to be reciprocated by the Spanish.

But the army at large was not in possession of the secrets of the Commanders, and the passing days were filled with suffering among the wounded and sick as well as anxiety among all. The hardships were increasing; the daily rains made the trenches where the men were lying rivers of water; under the strain, the unbearable heat and the rains by day and the chill of the nights, the men's vitality grew low and disease was disabling more than half the army. To make it worse, the supply departments had apparently broken down; food was scarce and poor, medical supplies were exhausted. There was deep concern among the soldiers; it seemed only a matter of days before there would be no army except in the hospitals; and yet there was constant expectation of orders for a new assault.

As the days of parley after parley between the generals passed, the troops continued to intrench upon the ridge, although the ordinary tools for digging trenches were sadly lacking, and bayonets and tin cans had to do duty for picks and shovels. Artillery was brought up and put in the best positions. Finally, several regiments of new troops, fresh from home, arrived. General Nelson A. Miles, the commanding general of the army, came, and his presence gave new confidence. Each night the regimental bands along the line played " The Star-Spangled Banner," and then every man stood, facing the flag in silence, with uncovered head. These were noble moments; the most unthinking became reverent and thoughtful as all realized the enormous responsibility to their homes and country which this strange situation had put upon those thinning ranks; they knew that they were there for the extension of the free institutions which the flag represented.

On the 9th and 10th of July, as the demand for surrender was still not complied with, there was some artillery fire upon the city, but it was not very severe; the city could not run away; its fate was settled. There was a strong desire to make the capture without destroying it or sacrificing more lives. Generous terms were offered to the Spanish. They were told they might retain their personal property and march out with honors. Finally it was agreed to send them to Spain. It was cheaper to do that than to guard and feed them here. It hastened the end, for the Spanish troops had suffered bitterly and were longing to go home.

On the 14th of July, General Wheeler, who was conducting the negotiations on the American side, on behalf of General Shafter, gave the soldiers definite intimations that a surrender was close at hand. Then General Miles, with his staff, left for Puerto Rico, that he might not seem to rob General Shafter of his due or take to himself any honors which his own fighting had not won. On the morning of the 17th, aides rode along the lines and invited the commanders of divisions and brigades, with their staffs, to repair to the head-

8

quarters of the commanding general and witness the surrender of the Spanish forces.

Soon, from the general headquarters, a company of generals with their staffs and orderlies, numbering perhaps two hundred in all, and a couple of troops of cavalry swung into the main road leading to Santiago. They appeared as they had appeared from the day of the landing, except that the tropical sun had deepened their tan, and the experiences of battle had marked deep lines upon their faces. Their rough uniforms bore the stains of service and of conflict. There was no effort at display in this American cavalcade. They were plain, hardy, earnest men, bent upon results, who cared nothing for show until the results were made secure. There was little exultation, for they were soldiers who were able to respect the desperate valor of the defense they had overcome.

Coming upon the field where the formal ceremony of surrender was to occur, General Toral, with his staff, rode forward to greet them, saluted, shook hands with courtesy, introduced strangers to each other, and then escorted the American officers down the Spanish lines. Polite, complimentary, even congratulatory words were spoken on both sides. The Spanish officers appeared in uniforms that were bright with gold braid, and they wore across their breasts the medals and decorations they had won. The Spanish soldiers were at their best. Even in the hour of defeat there were smiles and salutations. At this most trying time the Spaniards did not fail to show both the pride and

the fine air of politeness which are so characteristic of
the Latin races.

Then the mixed group of general officers took position, and the Spanish regiments began marching past
with their arms and equipments, deposited them at a
designated place, and marched back again without
them.   The number doing this, with those who soon
after came in from the surrounding country to surrender, was about twenty-three thousand.   After a
small portion of the enemy had laid down their arms,
the American officers, accompanied by the Ninth Infantry and a squadron of the Second Cavalry, rode
on into the city to take possession and to raise the
flag.

Along the way there were the evidences of hasty
retreat and of the horrors of war.   Quickly made and
shallow graves were numerous.   Dead horses with
saddles and bridles yet upon them were frequent.
Destruction and wretchedness were visible on every
side.

The company entered the city between long lines of
troops still bearing arms, and multitudes of people.
They were not unkindly, and appeared to enjoy a surrender better than an assault.   Doubtless the appearance was an honest representation of the general feeling,
for the citizens were glad to see the power of Spain
vanish; the Spanish officials must have been convinced
that subjugation of Cuba was impossible and that re-
sisting the United States was hopeless; and the Spanish soldiers were more than willing to get out of a

Raising the Flag over the Palace   The Cheers from the Trenches

conflict in which they never had much heart, and to see the prospect of getting home once more.

To the people, the coming of the American army meant food and security. A strong curiosity was clearly evident on each side to see what sort of people were on the other side, and this grew as the armies afterward mingled with each other.

Reaching the Plaza, or public square, the general officers were shown into the audience hall of the palace and received ceremoniously by the Spanish commander.

At noon the officers returned to the square, the troops presented arms, and as the clock pointed the hour of twelve, Captain McKittrick, of General Shafter's staff, raised "Old Glory" over the palace. The regimental band played "The Star-Spangled Banner," and a national salute of twenty-one guns announced to the army in the trenches on the hilltops, two miles away, and to the navy at the watery gateway of the city, that the flag was floating over Santiago in sign of the victory which they had together won. Those guns boomed a solemn declaration that henceforth government by the people must supplant the cupidity and the cruelty of Spanish rule in the Western Hemisphere.

The Capture of Puerto Rico

No sooner was the surrender of Santiago assured, than General Nelson A. Miles, the commanding officer of the Army of the United States, departed from Cuba with a few regiments of regulars and volunteers to take possession of the island of Puerto Rico.

This expedition had been long deferred in order that all danger from the Spanish warships, now destroyed, might be avoided. It was generally felt in the United States that, since Cuba was to have independence, Puerto Rico must be seized as partial indemnity for our enormous expenditures of money in prosecuting the war. Rear-Admiral Sampson, on the 12th of May, had spent a few hours in bombarding San Juan, the capital of the island, with a view of ascertaining the strength of its defenses, but had withdrawn his fleet to Cuba, since the military expedition for Puerto Rico was not at that time ready, and also because Admiral Cervera's fleet, for which he was searching, was yet on the seas and must be destroyed.

When General Miles's expedition started it was expected by the public, the newspapers, and even by the Government, that he would land on the north coast and make a short march to San Juan along the line of a well equipped railroad. But General Miles kept his counsels secret, and, to the surprise of everyone, even of the keen-scented newspaper dispatch boats, he suddenly, on the 28th of July, landed at Ponce, on the southern coast. He found some vessels of the American navy already there. They had, a few days before, captured Guanica at the southeastern end of the island, and had then sailed eastward a short distance to the city of Ponce, which was now in their power. The

formal surrender, however, was made to General Miles
when he entered at the head of his troops.

The people of Puerto Rico received the Americans
with open-armed hospitality. The Spanish rule had
been as deeply hated in Puerto Rico as in Cuba, but
as the people were of a less revolutionary temper, the
fire of insurrection had not swept the island. They
had, however, been expecting the American forces,
and were prepared to greet them with warm friendliness and to give hearty allegiance to the flag of the
great Republic of freedom.

Upon taking possession of the city, General Miles
issued a proclamation in which he said:

" In the prosecution of the war against the kingdom
of Spain by the people of the United States, for the
sake of liberty, justice, and humanity, its military
forces have come to occupy the island of Puerto Rico.
They come bearing the banners of freedom, inspired
by noble purposes, to seek the enemies of our Government, and yours, and to destroy or capture all in
armed resistance.

" The chief object of the American military forces
will be to overthrow the armed authority of Spain and
give the people of your beautiful island the largest
measure of liberty consistent with this military occupation.

" They have not come to make war upon the people
of the country, who for centuries have been oppressed,
but on the contrary to bring protection to yourselves
and your property, to promote your prosperity, and to

bestow the immunities and blessings of our enlightened institutions and liberal government. This is not a war of devastation, but one to give all within the control of the military and naval forces of the United States the advantages and blessings of enlightened civilization.''

The prisoners held by the Spaniards for political offenses were released. One who had cut the telegraph leading to the capital on the preceding night, in order to prevent the Spaniards from sending for reinforcements, was being led out by them to be shot just as the American ships entered the harbor. His captors departed with haste and left him a free man under a new flag. Then the regiments from Massachusetts, Pennsylvania, Illinois, and Wisconsin soon began patrolling the city and scouting through hiding-places in quest of lurking Spaniards.

The city of Ponce had enjoyed considerable prosperity, and many of the people were intelligent and well-to-do. They extended their hospitality to the American officers, and the troops found themselves greeted with smiles and cheers at every turn.

Homes were opened and Puerto Rican dainties were pressed upon the soldiers in the streets. At the first concert given by an American band in the Plaza the enthusiasm of the people at the new music resembled the enthusiasm with which, at home, the playing of patriotic music had been received when the soldiers were going to the front. It seemed as though the campaign was destined to be a huge picnic; certainly never before had a people manifested such joy and good-will at being conquered.

General Miles, however, did not relax his careful strategy and discipline. Though the Spanish troops had retired from Ponce, he knew they were massing toward San Juan, and were preparing for stubborn resistance. There were excellent roads from Ponce to San Juan, and along them were a number of strongly garrisoned towns. Notwithstanding the fact that the usual conditions seemed to be reversed, and the defenders instead of the invaders seemed to be in the enemy's country, General Miles arranged his advance on San Juan with the most painstaking skill. The army was to advance in three divisions along three different roads; careful reconnoissances were continually made, and no chances were taken.

But as the troops advanced, the Spanish withdrew after some desultory fighting in which they met with some losses, and a few were killed and wounded on the American side. A sharp little battle was fought at Coamo, where a detachment of the enemy surrendered after a desperate struggle in which most of their officers were killed. The Spanish army made a decisive stand on the 13th of August. General Brooke drew up his troops for an overwhelming attack. But just as the American General was about to give the order to the artillerymen to open fire upon the Spanish lines, Lieutenant Maclaughlin dashed up on a foaming horse with a dispatch from headquarters that the preliminaries of peace had been made and that no more

The Messenger of Peace, Puerto Rico, August 13, 1898.

fighting was to be done.   This order, at the beginning of what seemed to be an exceptionally brilliant and skillful campaign, was received with varying emotions by our soldiers.   Some were disappointed that they would not have the opportunity to emulate the valor of their comrades in Cuba; but more shared in the gratification of the American people that bloodshed was at an end.   When the news of the truce reached the Spanish lines their soldiers were seen to dance for joy.

This was the end of the fighting with Spain in the West Indies.   Our troops settled down in their camps among the friendly Puerto Ricans to await orders which should call them home, while the Commissioners appointed by the two contending Governments soon arranged for the evacuation of the island by the Spanish, whose robberies and cruel oppression had for so many centuries made the Spanish flag and uniform abhorrent.

CHAPTER X

Fall of Manila and the Suit for Peace

WHILE the gallant troops of the East under General Miles were capturing Puerto Rico, and while the veterans of the Santiago battles were recovering from the terrible rigors of that campaign, another army, composed chiefly of Western regiments, together with some seasoned regiments of the regular army, was preparing to take possession of the Philippine Islands.

It was on the 1st of May that Commodore Dewey had fought his battle and destroyed the Spanish naval power in the Pacific. But though he remained master of Manila Bay, the city and suburbs of Manila, with their three hundred thousand inhabitants, the great island of Luzon in which it was situated, and the other islands of the Philippine group, were still occupied by the Spaniards. Dewey had no trouble in maintaining his position in the harbor, and could at any time have captured the city of Manila if he had deemed it expedient. He preferred to postpone the capture of the city until the arrival of the American army of occupation. So he cut the cable from the island to Hong-Kong and made his sailors as comfortable as possible while waiting for reinforcements.

He was, however, recognized by the warships of the great powers which visited the bay as having full control, and the Spaniards in the city knew that they were at his mercy.

During the month of May a military expedition for the Philippines began to gather at San Francisco. Major-General Wesley Merritt, one of the most distinguished and able officers of the army, was put in command. While there was every reason for haste in starting the expedition on its thirty days' voyage across the seven thousand miles of the Pacific Ocean, General Merritt was too sensible an officer to send off his troops without a fully adequate equipment. Supplies of every kind, horses, mules, rations, fodder, clothing and blankets, medical supplies, in addition to arms and munitions of all kinds, had to be gathered at the Golden Gate. Many of these supplies came from the far East. Weeks were consumed in getting together the needful equipment. But as fast as a detachment was ready it was started on its adventurous voyage.

It was the first time in our history as a nation that our soldiers were sent over such an enormous distance. It began to seem to some people that these departing soldiers of the Republic might possibly be the first soldiers of an American empire, which, like Great Britain, would reach its arms to the other side of the world. Peculiar interest, therefore, attached to every departing ship as it pushed its way over the western horizon. The friends of the troops, moreover, realized that their soldier boys were to be separated from home by an entirely different kind of gulf from that which lay between the United States and Cuba and Puerto Rico.   Unknown perils, as well as a new kind of struggle in an unknown empire, were known to be lying ahead.

The voyage of the several detachments of the Philippine expedition was accomplished without accident. Hawaii was in the course of the transports bearing the troops, and the inhabitants of those islands, which had just been annexed by act of Congress, as they extended their welcome to our soldiers, were impressed with the power of the nation under whose flag the Hawaiian Islands had just come.

During July some eight thousand American soldiers arrived in Manila Bay, and General Merritt determined that these would be sufficient for the assault upon the Spanish fortifications and the capture of the city behind them.

The Spanish troops outnumbered the Americans, and, to add to the difficulty of the situation, there was encamped outside of Manila a large army of native insurgents under the command of General Aguinaldo.

These insurgent troops had been fighting the Spaniards ever since Dewey's victory and had driven them into their fortifications around the city.   Aguinaldo's soldiers were not our allies, though fighting a common foe; and what their attitude would be was an open and perplexing question both to General Merritt and to the Government at Washington.   The people of the Philippines had suffered as cruelly at the hands of the Spaniards as had the people of Cuba, and had been engaged in a desperate revolution against their oppressors. This revolution had been suppressed about a year before the breaking out of our war with Spain. But at the signal of Dewey's expedition against the Spanish fleet at Manila, Aguinaldo, a young, shrewd, and ambitious chief, assisted by Dewey, had organized the revolt anew; and now with a large army of natives, flushed with the fall of their enemy before American arms, he was a factor not to be forgotten.

The United States Government, however, did not feel itself warranted in undertaking the liberation of the Philippines and giving the control to the native population, who were ignorant, undisciplined, and as yet altogether unfit for self-government. Indeed a government of the islands by the Filipinos would be almost certain to be more oppressive and mistaken than by the Spaniards themselves. Consequently our commanders were debarred from making common cause with Aguinaldo. Yet, since he had with him at that time the sympathies of many of the natives, it was necessary to avoid, as much as possible, complications which might result in a conflict between his forces and the Americans.

Under these conditions, to conquer the Spanish army and to shoulder aside or ignore the insurgent army without engaging it in battle, constituted a problem which required diplomacy as well as generalship.

But difficult as the task was, General Merritt and his officers were equal to its solution.

General Merritt treated Aguinaldo not as an enemy, yet with unmistakable firmness. The American General did not seek the help of the insurgent leader, for he was unwilling to be under obligations to men who would naturally demand the right to sack the city and who would more than likely be jealous of the army which should take possession of it.

Some embarrassment was experienced by reason of the fact that Aguinaldo's forces, numbering several thousand men, occupied the ground between the landing-place of the American troops and Manila; but when General Merritt sent a request that they should get out of the way, they thought it well to do so, and thus gave the Americans open roads to the city.

Without waiting for the balance of the twenty thousand troops which were still on their way from San Francisco, General Merritt, by the end of July, began preparations to advance upon the city. On the night of the 31st of July the brigade of General F. V. Greene was thrown forward. It met with a sharp resistance from both the Spanish infantry and artillery, but held its ground valiantly.

On the 6th of August General Merritt and Rear-Admiral Dewey joined in a letter to the Spanish Captain-General notifying him to remove the women and children and the sick from the city within forty-eight hours, and that an attack was liable to be made at any moment after that time. Three days later a formal demand was made for the surrender of the city, which was met with a request for time and permission to send a boat to Hong-Kong, six hundred and forty miles distant, to cable the Spanish Government. This was refused, and it was decided to take the city four days later.

The seacoast batteries of the Spaniards were so situated as to make it impossible for our navy to engage them without firing into the city, and as the non-combatants had not been removed, it was desired, in the interest of humanity, to avoid this. So the duty of the assault fell largely upon the infantry of the army. It was necessarily delayed a day or two longer than intended, but was made according to programme on the 13th of August.

After days of inaction, during which the troops were encamped upon swampy ground under pouring rains, and had begun to think they would never see the inside of Manila, there came, on the 12th of August, the general order of advance. The troops were to move up into the trenches at half-past six the next morning, —the First Brigade, under General McArthur, on the right, and the Second Brigade, under General Greene, on the left and down the beach; the combined attack by sea and land was to take place on Saturday the 13th of August, at ten A.M.

The troops received the order with rejoicing. But as they eagerly pulled themselves out of the marshes, to fall in for the assault, there was no excitement; the volunteers were as cool as the regulars.

As the troops floundered on through the marsh and
the rain, the Utah Battery opened fire from its em-
brasures on the fort, San Antonio.   At the same time
the fleet commenced firing with its big shells, and
its barking rapid-fire guns from the military tops, with
upon the Spanish fortifications.   At a given signal, a
little later, the batteries and the fleet ceased firing, for
the infantry to make an assault.   A company of Colo-
rado volunteers had the honor of making the first advance at the fort.   When they arrived, before it was
destroyed, Lieutenant McCoy pulled down the flag of
Spain and sent up the Stars and Stripes.

Back of the fort lay the town of Malate, protected
by breastworks and sand-bags.   Our soldiers pushed
on over the second line of intrenchments.   Here they
met a sharp fire and a number fell.   During the advance there were many deeds of splendid gallantry.
One of these was when, in response to a call for volunteers to dislodge the enemy from a stubborn stand, the
men of the Astor Battery of New York volunteered
their services, and charged upon the Mauser rifles,
armed only with revolvers.   It was an unequal and
desperate chance, but they were supported by reinforcements and the Spanish fled.

The walled city of Manila was now in sight and a
white flag was seen.   Two officers, representing the
army and the navy, were sent in to negotiate the terms
of surrender.   There was the usual Spanish bickering,
but finally General Greene rode in and received the
surrender of the Captain-General, while our volunteers

Leslie W Lee-08

American Volunteers Entering Manila, August 13, 1898.

marched triumphant through the streets and raised the new colors above the ancient Spanish city.

Meantime the insurgents, who had been running along by a parallel road with our advance, began to jostle their way into the city with the idea of loot. They were, however, sternly held back, and, though they had forced their way into our lines, were driven out, to their bitter disappointment.

The capital of the Philippines was now in the hands of the United States. The resistance, though sharp, had been but feeble in comparison with what it might have been. The Spanish were glad to surrender, but they did not dare to return home without making at least a show of resistance. They recognized the hopelessness of further struggle against the North American race, and, though amply provided with ammunition and provisions, they were glad to have the struggle over.

Well might General Merritt, a splendid and modest soldier, close his report of the movement by saying: " I submit that for troops to enter under fire a town covering a wide area, to rapidly deploy and guard all principal points in the extensive suburbs, to keep out the insurgent forces pressing for admission, to quietly disarm an army of Spaniards, more than equal in numbers to the American troops, and, finally, by all this to prevent entirely all rapine, pillage, and disorder, and gain entire and complete possession of a city of three hundred thousand people, filled with natives hostile to American interests and stirred up by the knowledge that their own people were fighting in the outside trenches,—was an act which only the law-abiding, temperate, resolute American soldier, well and skillfully handled by his regimental and brigade commanders, could accomplish."

The taking of the capital of the Philippines was accomplished after the preliminary terms of peace had been accepted by the contending Governments, but before the instructions to cease hostilities could reach the American officers. Fortunately it was done without much bloodshed, but it would have been done at the appointed time no matter whether the loss was little or much. It gave the United States a real foothold on the other side of the world, and imposed upon the Republic unprecedented responsibilities, for it opened a door through which the American nation was constrained to pass, and to attempt to carry its power, its spirit, and its institutions into the affairs of the Oriental peoples.

Before the end of July (on the 25th) the French Ambassador at Washington called at the White House and stated to President McKinley and the Secretary of State that he was requested by the Government of Spain to say that " Spain has been worsted and that her sufferings, as a result, are very great, and, therefore, she asks to be furnished with a statement of the terms upon which the United States would be willing to make peace."

This was all that could be desired. It meant peace

and it sent a thrill of jubilant satisfaction throughout the country.

Some days were necessarily consumed in discussing details. There were exchanges of notes and of visits between the diplomats, and the European cables conveyed new questions and instructions daily. By the 12th of August the demands of the United States had been formulated and accepted by Spain in the following language:

" 1. That Spain shall relinquish all claim of sovereignty over and title to Cuba.

" 2. That Puerto Rico and other Spanish islands in the West Indies, and an island in the Ladrones, to be selected by the United States, shall be ceded to the latter.

" 3. That the United States shall occupy and hold the city, bay, and harbor of Manila pending the conclusion of a treaty of peace, which shall determine the control, disposition, and government of the Philippines.

" 4. That Cuba, Puerto Rico, and the other Spanish islands in the West Indies shall be immediately evacuated, and that Commissioners, to be appointed within ten days, shall, within thirty days from the signing of the Protocol, meet at Havana and San Juan, respectively, to arrange and execute the details of the evacuation.

" 5. That the United States and Spain shall each appoint not more than five Commissioners to negotiate and conclude a treaty of peace. The Commissioners are to meet at Paris not later than the first day of October.

" 6. On the signing of the Protocol hostilities shall be suspended and notice to that effect shall be given as soon as possible by each Government to the commanders of its military and naval forces."

On the same day President McKinley issued a proclamation declaring hostilities at an end. Upon the instant messages were sent by wire, and then by dispatch boats over the seas, to the navy, and by military couriers over the mountains to the army, that they should stay the iron hand of war. Directly Commissioners were appointed to adjust the details of the evacuation of Cuba and Puerto Rico by the Spanish armies, and other Commissioners to meet the Spanish representatives in Paris in order to negotiate and agree upon the terms of a general and permanent peace.

CHAPTER XI

The Spirit of American Soldiers and Sailors

IT was love of freedom and compassion for the oppressed which impelled the United States to make
war upon Spain for the liberation of the Cubans. The
American people were in advance of their Government
in this impulse. It was but right that the Government
should hesitate and wait for the clear manifestation of
the will of the people before taking a step so momentous and so unprecedented. But history will accord
to the people the just credit for moving to such a
generous and true-hearted undertaking by a common
impulse.

The response to the call of the Government for men
and money for the prosecution of the war was as prompt
as the popular impulse was enthusiastic. The President called for two hundred thousand men, and nearly
a million offered themselves. A popular loan of two
hundred millions of dollars was asked for, and more
than fourteen hundred millions were offered.

What is of no less account, wherever the soldiers and
sailors of the United States went, they carried the
spirit and the self-control of their people with them.
They were worthy representatives of a republic where

the people govern themselves, and they exemplified the virtue and the heroism of the Anglo-Saxon race.

In all their history the Spaniards have followed their conquests with pillage and outrages. Their soldiers have had license to plunder houses and rob and mal-treat their prisoners. Even in later times the Spanish soldier has calculated upon this permission, which has been accorded as a spur to greater daring in battle.

The Cubans and the Filipinos who were fighting Spain expected a somewhat similar license for them-selves if they gained the victory in their wars for inde-pendence. It is not strange, for they are for the most part an uneducated and almost an uncivilized people; they are but Spaniards themselves by origin, and have been trained in the thought, traditions, and practices of the Spanish nation. So when Santiago and Manila were taken, the army of the United States was obliged to use strategy and force to protect their own enemies, the Spaniards, and their property from such terrible outrages as they themselves have many times inflicted upon conquered cities.

General Shafter and General Merritt, in order to make certain that no wrong should be done, refused to permit the native soldiers to enter the cities which the Americans had taken. The insurgents were very angry at this; there were some fears that their dis-appointment and rage might even lead them to resist by force, and that before we were through we might have both sides to fight; but they were told to see in the firmness of the Americans the beginnings of justice as well as power. The United States was in their islands in the name of human liberty, and her troops were abundantly able to afford security and protection in the territory they had conquered.

In Cuba, affairs began to move in the usual ways, or indeed in much better than the usual ways, very soon. Civil government was reëstablished, business was resumed, the mails and the newspapers were started again; better still, the officers of the United States looked to the care of the sick, to the cleaning of the towns, and to the opening of schools. When Santiago was captured it was unspeakably filthy; it always had been notorious for its extreme dirtiness. General Wood immediately organized hundreds of hungry Cubans into a cleansing army; and in a few weeks Santiago passed to the other extreme of being, for a time at least, the cleanest city in the world. In Manila, it is said, the street cars were running and ladies were down street shopping in an hour after the American troops were in possession of the city. Some of the nations of Europe might wonder at this quick restoration of order; but to an American it was only natural to see American boys affording protection to the weak and representing the orderliness of their people, as well as the blessings of liberty, at their entrance upon foreign soil.

The treatment of prisoners was only what we knew it would be, yet the kindness and the generosity of it appeal to the pride and warm the heart of every American.

When Commodore Dewey destroyed the Spanish fleet in Manila Bay, the telegraph cable to Hong-Kong was cut before the reports of the battle were finished, so that the world was left for several days in some doubt as to the result. What information did come by wire was through Spanish officials. The last word received was that "the Americans had landed at Cavite to bury their dead." This led to the fear that the American vessels had met with a heavy loss. In fact they had met with no loss. They did land to bury the dead, but it was the Spanish dead. They also landed to give succor to the Spanish sick and wounded. The Spaniards seemed powerless to do what was necessary and were doubtless in fear of the insurgents. While our men were thus engaged there was a very singular occurrence.

When the party landed from the American fleet they were met by a procession of priests who came to present a humble prayer. It was that the Americans would "spare the sick and wounded." It was supposed that the sailors who were so heroic in battle had come to slay their fallen adversaries and pillage their possessions, when they had really come on an errand of mercy. How little they understood the American people, their feelings, and their ways!

When the desperate assault of the American troops at El Caney had finally triumphed, three young Spaniards were found in the blockhouse which through the long and terrible day had been one of the main targets of the American fire. Wounded, and exhausted by the intense heat and the want of food and drink, they were taken in pity to the quarters of General Chaffee for refreshment. When a lieutenant of the Seventeenth Infantry asked them if they would not have a drink of water he was amazed at the answer. The Spanish corporal said : " No, why should we drink when we are about to die ? " They had misconstrued the kindness, and expected to receive the treatment they would have been ready to give to the Americans if the circumstances had been reversed and if there had been anything to gain by it. The American lieutenant had no need to wait for instructions as to the reply he should make. He knew that every citizen of the United States would say as he did : " You are not to die ; we are civilized men and you are brave ones ; we have beaten you in a just cause, now we will help you."

The heroic bravery of American soldiers in the face of danger has come to be known all over the world. It shines through every page of the history of our warfare. Upon the sea and upon the land, in the Colonial wars, in the Revolution, in the Second War with Great Britain, in the Mexican War, and particularly in the Civil War, Americans demonstrated that they were willing to take any chances and would fight to the death. In the war against Spain, the sterling heroism, the brilliant intrepidity of the Americans seemed more marked than ever before ; the deep desire for an opportunity to risk his life in the cause seemed to have taken possession of nearly every man in the service. The place of greatest danger was the place earnestly pleaded for by almost every man in the army and the navy. Where such was the common spirit, when all were alike eager, it seems unjust to make distinction by naming individual heroes. Yet there were certain great deeds which deserve to be recounted, not so much to praise those who performed them, as because they were typical and to inspire other Americans to offer no less for their country and for humanity.

Admiral George Dewey, a Vermont boy, grew up in the navy. Though recognized as an efficient naval officer there seemed nothing very unusual about him. But the opportunity came to him to perform a great act of world-wide importance, and he had the fiber in him to seize it and make the most of it. In taking an American fleet, at night, into the close harbor of a city of three hundred thousand people, on the other side of the world, a harbor which he had never seen before and which was protected by submarine mines and shore batteries, and in which there was a fleet of enemy's vessels outnumbering his own, he performed an act of the highest personal gallantry. In utterly destroying that fleet and bringing that city to subjection he brought a distinguishing glory to the American navy, for it was a deed unprecedented in warfare upon the seas, and one which will live as long as history is written.

After the war broke out the War Department found it necessary to communicate with the leaders of the

Cuban insurrection. It was imperative to arrange for military coöperation. They were in the heart of Cuba, going from place to place in the mountains and in the forest, and could only be reached by a special messenger traveling hundreds of miles through an enemy's country. Such a mission called for rare judgment, involving immense hardship, and the capture of such a messenger would result in his certain death.

Lieutenant Andrew S. Rowan of the War Department was made happy beyond measure by being permitted to undertake the dangerous work. He went from New York by steamer to Kingston on the south shore of the island of Jamaica and there awaited instructions by cable from Washington. These he got on the 23rd of April, and started immediately across country to carry the news to the Cuban leaders and fulfill his even more important mission. He traveled seventy-five miles across this island in a northwesterly direction to the sea; crossed over to the Cuban shore, a distance of a hundred miles, in a small sailboat, avoiding all manner of Spanish craft; thence threaded his way another hundred miles through the thickets, guided by Cuban officers, sleeping in the brush, living on sweet potatoes and water from the green cocoanuts, until in the very midst of the jungle he reached the headquarters of the Cuban commander-in-chief.

It was the same day upon which Dewey destroyed the fleet at Manila. It was noon, and first he was given breakfast. Then the two men worked together until dark. In the meantime Lieutenant Rowan had given what information he had and secured what there was to get. He left upon his return an hour after nightfall. He carried papers upon his person, both in going and in returning. He had not been engaged in corrupting an officer of the enemy or in furthering the designs of a traitor, but aside from this was in precisely the same situation that Major André was when arrested by American soldiers in the Revolution. If taken he would have met the same fate, probably without trial and with less deliberation. He had to travel more than another hundred miles before reaching the northern coast of Cuba. Here he secured a rowboat from Cuban sympathizers. A sail was made from hammock canopies, and food was gathered from the forests.

In this frail craft he started at night, with five Cubans, over the treacherous southern seas, for Nassau in the Bahamas, a distance of two hundred miles or more. In time he gained his port, soon got a steamer for Key West, and hastened by the first train to Washington to deliver his report and papers to the commanding general of the army. General Miles immediately wrote a letter to the Secretary of War saying: " Lieutenant Rowan performed an act of heroism and cool daring that has rarely been excelled in the annals of warfare," and recommended that he be promoted to the position of lieutenant-colonel.

When the Spanish fleet under Admiral Cervera was blockaded in Santiago Bay, Admiral Sampson con-

The Merrimac Entering Santiago Harbor, June 3, 1898.

ceived the idea of making the blockade doubly sure by placing an obstruction in the mouth of the narrow entrance so that no ship could pass. The channel was but about three hundred and fifty feet wide and such an obstruction, rightly placed, would close it altogether.

During the run of the flagship from Key West to join the blockaders at Santiago, the Admiral, with young Naval Constructor Richmond Pearson Hobson, perfected a plan for doing this. It was to take the collier Merrimac, loaded with coal, into the mouth of the harbor, drop her anchors, shatter her hull with small torpedoes, and sink her lengthwise across the opening. The collier was nearly as long as the width of the channel. If this could be done it would relieve in some measure the vigilance of the blockading squadron and perhaps allow some of the vessels to be withdrawn for needed service elsewhere. But if it was to be undertaken it would have to be by cool-headed and heroic men taking their lives in their hands. The old vessel would require to be taken into the fire of the shore batteries and of the Spanish fleet, and then the men, if any still lived, would have to leave her. Detection was certain and the possibility of escape with life was exceedingly remote.

The bright naval constructor was given the coveted honor of carrying out the plan which he had largely developed. He was a young man from Alabama, twenty-seven years of age. He graduated at the Naval Academy in the class of '89, being the youngest member and standing at the head of his class.

After some sea service he gave his closest attention to construction of vessels. He was sent to Europe to study, and afterwards proposed and conducted a postgraduate course in naval architecture at the Academy at Annapolis. He had already shown himself to be a gentleman, a student, and an adept at practical affairs. Now he was to prove that he was a hero.

Six men were wanted to assist him in his perilous undertaking, and volunteers were called for. On the flagship New York alone, three hundred men asked for leave to go and give their lives, if it should be so, to their country's service; a proportionate number responded upon each of the other vessels; indeed nearly every man in the fleet was ready. The six men selected were Daniel Montague, George Charette, J. C. Murphy, Oscar Diegnan, John P. Phillips, and John Kelly. Rudolph Clausen from the New York also remained on board of the Merrimac, longing to be one of the party, and was finally allowed to go.

It was arranged that they should enter the harbor at about half-past three on the morning of the 2nd of June. At that hour the tide would be running in, the moon would have set, and there would be an hour and a half of darkness before daylight. But after working well through the night, they could not get the collier ready in time and started a little late; consequently Admiral Sampson called them back and directed them, much to their disappointment, to wait until the next morning.

On the following morning, accordingly, all being

ready, they started in just after moonset, and half an hour before dawn. The gallant little crew were dressed in nothing but their underclothes and life-preservers; each had a revolver strapped to his waist. Every vessel in the American fleet was on the alert; every man's nerves were at the highest tension over the success of the project and the fate of his comrades. Thousands of eyes peered through the gloom to watch the old collier approach the mouth of the harbor and disappear. The scene was quickly lighted by the sheets of fire from Morro Castle and the other batteries upon the shores. It seemed impossible for human life to exist at all in that deadly and concentrated fire. The watching crews dared hope no more than that the Merrimac was in position across the channel before she sank. The steam-launch of the New York, which had followed the Merrimac to pick up the crew if possible, was seen to attract the fire of the big guns; in time she steamed back to the flagship without any of the eight men. Her young commander, Cadet Joseph W. Powell, of Oswego, New York, a pupil and friend of Lieutenant Hobson, reported to the Admiral that he had been unable to find any of them. He had gone close under the batteries and waited until all hope of rescue had to be abandoned.

But as by miracle the men of the expedition had not perished. Having steered the ship to the appointed spot, Hobson gave the orders which should result in her being swung across the channel and sunk. But in the downpour of shot and shell the Merrimac's rudder

had been shot away and also her stern anchor; moreover the electric batteries were so damaged that only
part of the torpedoes attached around the hull could
be exploded.   Consequently, instead of sinking where
intended, the vessel drifted rudderless with the tide
far past the narrow neck.   But she was sinking steadily;
her own torpedoes and the enemy's shells had opened
her sides, and the water was rushing in.

According to the carefully arranged plans, the
crew were to leap into the water as the vessel sank,
and swim to the rowboat in tow; if the boat was damaged there was the life-raft on deck.   But the fire was
so incessant and sweeping, and so lighted was the scene
by the continuous flash, that it would have been madness at that close range for the crew to show themselves for an instant.   So Hobson made his men lie flat
on deck and wait for the ship to sink, or for the fire
finally to cease and for Spanish officers to whom they
could surrender to approach.   It was a terrible waiting
while every great gun and the Mauser rifles of the
soldiers were pouring their fire upon the ship, and the
decks around the devoted band were being torn by
the plunging shell.   At last the end came.   With a lift
and a fall the ship went under the waves.   Through
the whirlpool of rushing waters the men rose to the
surface and gathered around the life-raft, which was
floating, anchored still to the sunken ship.

Every man was there.   The existence of that unbroken company was the greatest marvel of the entire
war.   But there was no time for wondering then.   The

Spanish boats were now prowling about, and had one man been seen, all would have been shot. So they clung to the raft, only their faces out of the water, and waited for daylight.

When day finally broke, a steam-launch approached, bearing, as could be seen, an officer of high grade. To the men on this boat Hobson shouted: " Is there any officer on that boat to receive the surrender of prisoners of war ? " The sailors aimed their rifles, but they were dropped at a command and an elderly man raised his hand to Hobson.

It was Admiral Cervera. The Americans were taken to the Spanish flagship, and in the afternoon Admiral Cervera sent an officer under flag of truce to Admiral Sampson, telling him that they were safe, and adding: " Daring like theirs makes the bitterest enemy proud that his fellow-men can be such heroes." In a day or two the newspapers in both hemispheres were filled with the wonderful details of their exploit, and their countrymen throughout the United States were congratulating each other that American heroism had added such a new and extraordinary instance to its annals.

Two volunteers peculiarly interesting to the people, because of their previous eminence and well-known character, were General Joseph Wheeler and Colonel Theodore Roosevelt.

General Wheeler was over seventy years of age and in delicate health. In his youth he had been one of the most dashing and successful cavalry generals in the Confederate army, and during his later years he had been an honored congressman from Alabama. At the outbreak of the war with Spain, the venerable Southerner offered his sword to the President, who made him a major-general; and, under General Shafter in the Santiago campaign, he went from a sick-bed to the firing line, and displayed such activity, intrepid will, and wise generalship as to win the loving admiration of the entire country.

Colonel Roosevelt enlisted against the decided wish of the President and many of the people, who felt that in his place as Assistant-Secretary of the Navy he would be of far more value to the nation than on the field. But Roosevelt had long foreseen the war and had openly favored it. Moreover, he had long urged upon young Americans the duty of offering their lives to the country in time of danger. Consequently, when war was declared no dissuasion could restrain him, and, under his friend Colonel Wood, he was made lieutenant-colonel of the First Regiment of the National Volunteer Cavalry. This position was given him in recognition of his personal experience among the rough riders of the plains. It was his good fortune to win for himself and his gallant followers brilliant credit first at Guasimas and then at San Juan where, on horseback, revolver in hand, he led in the historic charge up that fire-swept slope.

Those two men—one aged and frail, the other young and robust, and both nobly distinguished in civil life

Richmond P. Hobson, Naval Constructor, U.S.N.

General "Fighting Joe" Wheeler

—illustrated in themselves the patriotic devotedness of the highest type of the American citizen.

The general testimony is that in the Santiago campaign there was comparatively little swearing and scarcely any grumbling. When men were on the firing line, marching or intrenching by night and fighting by day, and were without food, there was no complaining. The worst sufferers would say, " The Government is doing the best it can." The wounded had no fault to find at the delay of the surgeons and usually proposed that they should " help the other fellow first." Captain Arthur Lee of the British army, who was present for military study, tells of coming upon two men severely wounded, one of whom had been shot through the stomach. This man, when asked how he felt, answered with difficulty, " Oh, I am doing pretty well, sir." His companion suggested that the captain might find a doctor to help his friend, and the dying hero said : " That 's all right, Nick ; I guess the doctors have more than they can do looking after them as are badly hurt, and they will be along soon."

Mr. Stephen Bonsal, the correspondent, has narrated a tale of the stirring and characteristic heroism of young Lieutenant Ord and two boy privates who were with him in the charge upon San Juan. This is his story :

Just after the top of the hill had been triumphantly reached, and while it was still being swept by the

Spaniards' fire from a distance, Lieutenant Ord saw a wounded Spanish soldier on the very ridge and exposed to the bullets of his own comrades. Turning to two of his men, he said, " Take that Spaniard and carry him behind the blockhouse, out of the fire." The wounded man raised himself up, drew his revolver, and fired it full in Ord's face, killing instantly the gentleman who was trying to save his stricken enemy and showing a rarer grace of thoughtfulness than even that of Sir Philip Sidney, who, when wounded, gave his own cup of water to a wounded comrade.

When Lieutenant Ord, at the head of his men, started on the rush up the hill, there was by his side a boy private from Ohio, who had joined the regiment just before it had left for the front. He ran close to Ord until he fell, mortally wounded, a few yards from the summit. Ord heard him give a faint cry, and paused in his rush to say kindly as he saw the dying pallor on the boy's face, " My poor fellow, I can do nothing for you."

" I did n't call you back for anything like that, Lieutenant—I am done for, but I thought you had better take my steel nippers. There may be still another wire fence beyond that hill and I won't be there to cut it for you."

The boy private was a worthy comrade for his chivalrous officer, and he did not die until he heard the shout of victory; but he never knew that his gallant leader, to whom he had given such unselfish devotion, was lying dead not many yards away.

The third of that trio was even younger, and he, happily, did not have to die. He was a little flute-player, and was found sitting by the body of Lieutenant Ord, whom he had followed that day with manly daring and devotedness. Another officer came by and scolded him for sitting at a spot which was no place for children, and ordered him back to the hospital.

" I was going back," said the little boy. " I wanted to go back to the hospital and look after Colonel Egbert when he fell wounded, and I was doing no good at the front, for my flute is ruined with the mud and the rain. But just as I started back I heard Mr. Ord say, ' Now, all the boys who 's brave will follow me ; all the boys who 's brave, follow me ! ' and then he rushed ahead and kept that up for about half an hour, resting a little while and then rushing ahead. And every time he started up, he would shout back, ' Now, all the boys who 's brave will follow me ! ' So all the boys followed him, and as I was lighter I got farther ahead than most."

A cavalry colonel, who had just seen his own son die, listened to the little fellow's narrative, and, patting his shoulder, said with a smile of pleasure, " Ah, yes, there are many brave boys left, and you will make a good soldier some day."

One of the correspondents on the Brooklyn, Mr. George E. Graham, who is himself a highly courageous boy well known to the writer, said that, during the heat of the fight with Cervera's fleet, a shell got wedged into one of the guns on the side of the ship engaged with the enemy.   Instantly Corporal Robert Gray of the Marine Corps crawled out on the gun's muzzle, rammer in hand, to drive the shell out.   The gun was so hot he could not retain his hold and dropped down to the sea ladder.   There with the water beneath him and the frightful blast of the great guns above him, and with the shot of the enemy plunging around him, he renewed the attempt, but could not dislodge the shell.   Gunner Smith then tried it, but he too failed.   Then Private MacNeal of the gun squad asked and received permission to try it.   Clinging to the hot gun, with death by water assured if he dropped or was knocked off by concussion, and with the enemy firing at him, he got the rammer in the muzzle and rammed out the shell.   The men cheered and the gun continued to do its duty.   None of these men thought they had done anything unusual.   When, a few minutes later, a shell crashed into the compartment just below them they laughed at the Spanish gunner's aim.

Mr. Graham photographed a man in the act of replacing the flag at the masthead of the Brooklyn after it had been shot away.   The fire of the enemy was deadly all about him.   He did his work completely amid the cheers of the crew and came down the mast. As he landed on the deck the correspondent asked his name.   He declined to give it and disappeared in the crowd.

Less assistance than expected was obtained from the Cubans; but many were daring and at least one of them showed that he had his wits with him as well. " Shorty " Gonzales was a Cuban scout carrying dispatches over the hills, through the enemy's country, on mule-back, for American officers. Finding that he was certain to be captured by the Spaniards, he took from his pocket his rubber tobacco-pouch, put his dispatches in it, and forced the whole thing down the mule's throat. The Spaniards searched him, found nothing, concluded that he was only an ordinary Cuban countryman, and let him go. " Shorty " went on to his destination, killed the mule, and delivered his papers. He got great credit for his heroism and his wit; perhaps the mule ought to have some commendation too.

The daring and endurance of the newspaper men were no less marked than those of the soldiers.

The leading newspapers and magazines sent their correspondents to the battle front. They were allowed upon the war vessels, and they rented dispatch boats and went everywhere in quest of news. No expense was spared. Hundreds of thousands of dollars were expended in taking photographs and getting the latest news. Many newspapers issued a dozen editions a day and a few of them many more than that. The young men who gathered the news at the scenes of conflict were not only accomplished writers but they were heroic characters. They took their lives in their hands to discharge their duty to their newspapers and the people, no less than the sailors and the troops did. They freely assumed all the hazards of the dangerous service. They were frequently under fire and several of them were severely wounded. Without rest, without comforts, without fear, they reported the dreadful scenes of war more thoroughly and quickly than the work was ever done before.

There were heroic women as well as heroic men in the service.

The nurses of the Red Cross under the able lead of Miss Clara Barton carried food, medicines, and delicacies where the carnage was worst. In any event they would have been angels of mercy in perilous work; but, because of the weakness and demoralization in the regular medical department, and on account of the rapid advance of fevers among the troops in Cuba, they were almost imperative to the saving of the army. Their presence brightened the scenes of indescribable misery which followed the fighting, and their aid to the sick and wounded saved hundreds of lives. Opposed and not wanted at first by the medical department of the army, very soon, by their helpfulness and simple, direct way of giving relief, they turned opposition into welcome, and criticism into the most cordial coöperation. They came at the nick of time, and the military surgeons admit the enormous value of their labor of love for the sick and wounded. It was a patriotic and heroic service which the troops and the people will always hold in grateful memory.

While it was the intention to point out in this chapter only a few typical cases of great heroism in the face of personal danger, it is impossible to omit the name of President McKinley. Without encountering the danger of the battlefield, he exhibited moral heroism which required even higher courage. A veteran of the Civil War, he knew and dreaded the horrors of war. Of a kindly nature, he sympathized deeply with the Cubans. He hoped to avert war and to remove the oppression through diplomacy. Yet if war were to come, he felt that it must be because the sympathies and the conscience of the nation demanded it. If we were to take the unprecedented step of commencing a foreign war for the purpose of helping others, it must be the act of a united people. Diplomacy failed, and then the sentiment of the country unmistakably demanded that the Government should use force.

While he was holding back from the final act, he was accused by the unthinking and radical newspapers as lacking in decision. But all men afterwards comprehended that his seeming hesitation was the bravest and wisest statesmanship, for he knew the need of delay. Each day of waiting the people grew more united in supporting the war; every day of postponement made the army and navy more ready. Yet it required a supreme moral courage to withstand the reckless and often insolent urgency of those who loudly demanded an instant movement.

When the time for action came, the President was

the center of control, and the invigorating force of all acts of warfare. Events proved that while striving for peace he was preparing for war. Throughout the struggle he was steady, patient, kindly, vigorous, and unyielding,—a truthful exemplification both of the American character and of the American feeling regarding the war. Intensely patriotic, without an ill-timed partisanship, sorrowing with the distressed, believing in the justice and appreciating the dignity of our course, seeing the instant need of great energy and of overwhelming force in action, he gave power to the arm of the nation and then tempered its blows with mercy. He not only represented the best thought of the people of the United States, but he did it so wisely and so effectively as to be entitled without dispute to lead among the heroes.

In a word, the war of the United States against Spain was the war of the American citizen, breathing the spirit of his country, against a nation which once dreamed of ruling the world, but which has held back with arrested progress for three hundred years, while the neighboring nations have been advancing. It was made by a people filled with human sympathy and the spirit of progress, against a people characterized by an incorrigible hardness of heart and a persistent rapacity which have proved their ruin. The war would not have been made if Spain's atrocities had not been perpetrated upon a weak people at our very doors. The crimes at last became intolerable to a nation of freemen.

The Fury of a Just Indignation   not Understood by Spain

When the indignation of the people forced the Government of the United States into a foreign war, the people were ready to fight it out, regardless of cost in treasure or blood, to the bitter end. They offered themselves for service in the army and navy in hundreds of thousands. When they went into battle it was with a fury that was terrible.

Righteous indignation, in a just cause, has made the hardest fighters and the most sympathetic conquerors in all history. Spain was incapable of understanding either the force with which we gave her battle or the kindness with which we treated her defeated armies.

CHAPTER XII

The Results

THE Peace Commission met in Paris at the beginning of October. The American Commissioners were the Hon. William O. Day, of Ohio, who had just resigned the office of Secretary of State; Senator Cushman K. Davis, of Minnesota, Chairman of the Committee on Foreign Affairs in the Senate; Senator William P. Frye, of Maine; Senator George Gray, of Delaware; and the Hon. Whitelaw Reid, of New York.

Spain was represented by an equal number of eminent statesmen. The proceedings of this Commission were marked with a distinguished dignity and courtesy. The basis of the deliberations was the protocol of peace, which was given on pages 145, 146. The Spaniards, however, prolonged the discussions from day to day by raising objections, and by trying to prove by ancient precedents that the American demands were unusual; they also sought to induce other powers to exert diplomatic influence upon the Americans to swerve them from their purpose. But our Commissioners had definite instructions and they followed them without deviation; they were courteous but firm.

This straightforward American diplomacy was a surprise both to the Spaniards and to other European diplomatists, who were not accustomed to the simple and direct methods of the Americans in saying precisely what they meant and holding to it. Finally, after many weeks of discussion, a treaty of peace was arranged, which received the signatures of all the Commissioners.

This treaty, which was then carried back to the two respective Governments for ratification, was in brief as follows:

Spain relinquished all title and sovereignty to Cuba.

Spain ceded to the United States Puerto Rico and other Spanish possessions in the West Indies, excepting Cuba, together with the island of Guam in the Ladrones.

Spain ceded the Philippines to the United States on the payment of $20,000,000 by our Government, as indemnity for actual improvements.

Spain agreed to release prisoners held for political offenses in Cuba and in the Philippines.

Spain agreed to guarantee religious freedom in the Caroline Islands, assuring the rights of American missionaries there.

The United States agreed to send the Spanish troops, who were evacuating the Philippines, back to Spain.

The United States pledged to preserve order in the Philippines pending the ratification of the treaty.

Both Governments agreed to release all military prisoners and to relinquish indemnity claims.

Certain proposals by the United States as to the acquisition of territory in the Caroline Islands were left for future negotiations, after friendly relations had been resumed.

The United States agreed to inaugurate in the Philippines a generous commercial policy towards Spain.

These were the chief provisions. There were no demands made by the Americans which were not clearly defined or involved in the protocol, to which both Governments had previously agreed; yet the Spaniards had allowed themselves to hope that easier terms might be obtained through personal influence and arguments, and were accordingly disappointed at the firmness of the Americans.

But when the cause and purpose of the war and its accomplishment are fully held in mind, the demands of the United States seem neither large nor unjust.

The United States commenced war to liberate Cuba. The serious and unprecedented step was taken because of the natural sympathy of a free people with neighbors struggling for liberty. That sympathy was stronger because of the character Spain had borne among the nations. Yet no nation before had ever gone to war for the sole purpose of helping another people; so there were both deliberation and hesitation. The destruction of an American battleship, on a visit of peace, causing the death of more than two hundred and fifty American sailors, in the harbor of a people believed to be capable of treachery, was a definite summons to the nation to investigate seriously the whole situation at

once, to learn all the facts, and to demand that what was right should be done.

On investigation it was learned that proceedings hardly less merciless than those practiced by the Duke of Alva in the Netherlands in the sixteenth century were in truth going on at our very doors. They were being perpetrated by the same nation and for the same purpose now as then. A self-respecting people could not permit these things in its presence, any more than a man of honor can see a ruffian strike a woman without interposing. Protests were made, but without avail. Indignation finally outran diplomacy. The impulse to war was so general that, notwithstanding the fact that it was deplored by all and opposed by many, it was really a national feeling, and once aroused it could not be stemmed; the declaration of war was deliberate; the solemn act of war rested upon a sense of duty and of righteousness. The amazing results of the war surprise none more than ourselves, and are certain to be very far-reaching.

No one doubted our power to drive Spain out of Cuba; but the rapidity and the completeness with which it was done astonished the world. If there was some halting of sentiment in the country about commencing the war, there was none about prosecuting it. The spirit of the whole nation was united, without regard to party, and in three months we had broken the power of Spain in the West Indies and had island empires in both oceans upon our hands, with claims upon our generosity and our sense of right.

Wealth and resources are prodigious elements in modern warfare. There was no uncertainty about getting money; the only question was about spending it to the best advantage, and soon enough to satisfy the people. On the day of the declaration of war, the cash balance in the Treasury of the United States was $224,-541,637. The States were ready with *their* treasuries. The people were anxious to loan the Government thousands of millions at a low rate of interest. The only regret was that we had not expended more for the equipment of the army and navy and done it earlier.

The cost of warfare is enormous. A few items are suggestive. The cost of the battleship Oregon was $3,791,777. The Secretary of the Navy has said that the cost of supplying our warships with one full equipment of ammunition was $6,500,000. The coal bill of Admiral Dewey for the month of April was $81,872.91, and when he entered the harbor of Manila his vessels carried powder and shot and shell costing more than $1,000,000. Every time his ships completed the circle in the famous battle they fired ammunition costing over $100,000. The cost of a thirteen-inch gun is over $80,000. During the war the Government rented four great ocean-liners at $10,000 per day. These amounts are only random instances of the unusual expenses of war; the aggregate is startling. The Government actually paid out an average of $861,000 on account of the war each day of its continuance, and resulting claims will continue to accrue for fifty years.

The nations of Europe were impressed by the prompt-

ness of our financial support of the war.   Americans,
however, had their eyes opened to the danger of un-
readiness and were annoyed that so much of the
preparation had to be made after the outbreak.   They
were mortified at the inefficiency of the supply and
medical departments of the army, and there was a wide
demand that there should be a reorganization of the
army; that it should not only be enlarged, but that
professional soldiers rather than politicians should administer its affairs, and that military and technical
schools should be more generously supported.

One of the surprises of the war, to other nations, was
the competency of our professional officers and the
spirit of our soldiers and sailors.   The accuracy of our
gunners, and the tremendous effectiveness of our battleships were marvels to them, for they had no idea either
of the native ingenuity of our people or of the telling
effect which our technical schools are having upon
national skill.   The enthusiastic bravery of our soldiers
also, which was no surprise to us, seems to have been
unexpected by those peoples who do not read history,
or else do not comprehend the qualities of the Anglo-
Saxon race,—qualities which are stimulated further by
the peculiar conditions of American life.   It was known
to Americans that the Spaniards were fighters; but
they did not seem to believe that we were.   They were
surprised that our battleships and even our converted
pleasure yachts fought at close quarters with a fury they
had never considered possible in battle, and that our soldiers crawled nearer to them after every deadly volley.

Another of the surprises of the conflict was that in
the campaign in Cuba we had so little aid from the
Cubans. It must be allowed that they made very
weak allies. But they were of another race and the
greater part of them were unable to understand the
steady nerve and the businesslike habits of their American rescuers. The systematic way in which they have
been deceived and robbed, in which their homes have
been laid waste, and their wives and children starved
by the Spanish Government has had its unhappy influence upon their lives. They were not without
courage, for they had defied a Spanish army of two
hundred thousand men for several years; but they
were not in the same class with the American soldiers.
They could deliver a harassing blow and then get out
of the way, but they could not advance and continue
to advance upon intrenchments in the face of inevitable
slaughter.

But we had expected too much. In stature, in
qualities which make for manhood, in military equipment, and in general effectiveness their unorganized
forces seemed mean in comparison with American regiments. But we are to remember also that if this had
not been so, they would hardly have needed our help.
That they were worthy of freedom there is no question,
for they have suffered in fighting for it more than any
other modern people; and that they eventually will
profit by it there is every reason to hope. But one of
the results of the war is the insight we have gained as
to their real qualities, their still undeveloped capaci-

ties for self-government, and the kind of treatment they require.

One of the happy consequences of the war is the extent to which it developed a new spirit of union among the American people, as nothing else has done since the commencement of the bitter sectional contest over slavery. When the call came for a warlike patriotism and an unbroken front against a foreign foe, the old differences between the North and the South seemed to disappear; men who had waged deadly battle against each other in the last generation fought side by side with enthusiastic, fraternal regard. In stopping oppression and in helping others toward freedom, they gained new attachments for each other and new devotion to their common country.

One of the most gratifying and unexpected effects of the war has been an improved relation with Great Britain. British statesmen were outspoken in their commendation of our course, and the British Government went as far as a neutral power could in giving us every practicable encouragement. More important than that was the fact that the people of the two countries evidently found a new liking for each other. The mother country rejoiced in our victories, for we are of one blood, and she felt as if they were her own; she also seemed delighted at our departure from the old policy of isolation and our beginning to reach out to bear a hand in the affairs of the whole world. We on our part, warmed by this earnest friendliness and appreciation, began to see that our earlier enmities toward her, though natural once, had been cherished too long. Both nations came to perceive how much more there was in their common blood, language, traditions, tendencies, and beliefs to draw them together than there was in their old differences to divide them; both appeared to have much pleasure in realizing how much they might do, by acting together, to make the freedom, the justice, and the invigorating influences of the Anglo-Saxon race dominant throughout the whole earth.

Doubtless the most notable result of the course of the United States was this entrance, unintentionally, into the affairs of the Old World, through the unexpected acquisition of the Philippine Islands with their seven millions of people. The effect of our presence upon the resources and the development of those undeveloped islands must be very great, but it will be no less marked upon the national life of the United States and our relations with other nations and the common life of the world.

The words of the declaration of war clearly asserted the purpose of the United States to drive the power of Spain out of Cuba, to restore peace to the island, and then leave it to her people to establish a government of their own. It was our compassion for their sufferings, more than our faith in their political capacities, that impelled us.

At the time of the declaration of war, nothing more was thought of than to expel their oppressors and then to let them start for themselves. But later and better knowledge of the Cubans raises a very serious doubt about their being as yet properly qualified for self-government, or being able to maintain a stable government among themselves. We have taken the responsibility of freeing them from Spain; we are equal to the responsibility of deciding whether they are capable of governing themselves. If they can maintain government as we understand the term,—that is, if they can give security to persons and property, assure religious toleration, and guarantee freedom of thought and expression,—our specific obligations to them are at an end; if not, then we shall have to continue to regard ourselves as their guardians. We are bound to accomplish what we undertook. We not only undertook to expel Spain, but also to see that a full opportunity for self-government was assured. We are not to allow Spain to return, or another power to set up monarchical rule at our door; nor can we permit anarchy.

No question, however, about annexing Cuba or absorbing her people into our citizenship is yet to be met. That is not to be done except by the will of the Cuban people acting through a government of their own, or through a general election by citizens who can vote with reasonable intelligence.

Nor is it to be done even then, unless the Government of the United States thinks it well. Until Cuba can set up a government of her own, we are bound to protect her, and, so far as we can, to send to her schools and missionaries, books and newspapers, and the other instrumentalities of moral and intellectual progress, so that her people may develop to the point where they can manage their own affairs.

Puerto Rico and the islands of the Philippine Archipelago, with two or three others, have been acquired by cession in the treaty of peace. The taking of Puerto Rico was expected and was settled by the protocol agreed to by the two nations at the time of the ending of hostilities in August. The holding of the Philippines was a later matter about which there was difference of opinion in the United States, although it seemed to be desired by the more general sentiment of the country.

The capital of the Philippine Islands fell into the hands of the armed forces of the United States by an act of war. The capture of a seat of government has special significance in international law; it is considered to carry with it the territory of which it is the capital city. Military occupation of the capital is deemed to be military occupation of the whole country. In this case it was clearly evident that Spanish government in the whole archipelago of twelve hundred islands was at an end unless restored by the act of the United States. Such an act would have been clearly unjust to the heavily oppressed natives.

There were not a few Americans who thought it unwise and improper to hold the islands, because, as they said, they did not belong to us; their people were incapable of self-government and could not assimilate with us; we could not govern them without great expense and without bringing corrupt influences into our own affairs; and also because their possession would be in violation of the Constitution and plan of our government, and would inevitably involve us in turmoil with those European nations which are trying to increase their territory by taking new lands in the far East.

The reasons advanced by people of a different view, who insisted upon holding the islands, were as follows:

1. That they were but a proper indemnity for the cost of the war, and that by universal usage the defeated nation must make the expense good. At the close of the last war between France and Germany, the former was required to cede provinces and also to pay $1,000,000,000. After the war between China and Japan, the former had to give up Formosa and pay an indemnity of $168,000,000. When the short but fierce war between Greece and Turkey had ended, the Turkish frontier was extended and Greece was made to pay $20,000,000. But Spain had no money to pay. It was argued, accordingly, that the retention of the group was but right, and that the giving of $20,000,000 to Spain for any permanent improvements she had made there was an act of unprecedented generosity.

2. That the islands were commercially important; were rich in undeveloped resources; that we would develop them while Spain would not; that they were upon the natural highways of trade from our Pacific seaports to those of China and Japan, and thus would be a place of rendezvous for American merchants in the development of trade with those countries.

3. That they were necessary for military purposes;

that we must enlarge our power upon the seas, and possession of them would aid us in doing it.

4. That it would open the way for the evangelisation of their pagan people. Only one church was operating there, and the general missionaries had less opportunities than in China or Japan or even in Africa. The Gospel should be preached by representatives of all the denominations, and religious liberty must be enforced. This could be assured only by the United States.

5. That unless the American occupancy was made permanent, civil turmoil would continue. Spain could not govern them even if the United States withdrew. Conditions as bad as those which we commenced the war to relieve in Cuba would ensue.

6. That the Governments of Europe looked favorably upon our holding them, and that the Government and people of Great Britain desired it; that we could not do less without disappointing the expectations of the foremost nations of the world.

7. That we were bound to establish free institutions where American soldiers had, against armed resistance, carried the American flag; that having the opportunity we must carry the means of intellectual and moral progress to the millions of Filipinos; that it is the habit and the business of the Anglo-Saxon race to advance and aggressively exert its mighty influence in aid of mankind and in shaping the destiny of the world.

8. That the time had come when our national interests required that we should take our place among

the nations and assume our part in managing the affairs of the whole world; that by so doing the world's respect for us would be enlarged and the good influences of democratic government be increased ; that we were abundantly able to do all this, and should suffer if we hesitated; that the way would be made clear to us if we advanced, and that added strength would come to us if we obeyed the impulses of our Saxon, Dutch, and Norman blood and went manfully forward.

These are the considerations which led our Administration, following the public wish, to demand the Philippine Islands, and which led the Senate to ratify the treaty.

The " consent of the governed " is always a matter of prime importance with Americans, and so, some raised the question whether we had a moral right to set up our own rule over the Philippines when the natives had not given their consent. If the great body of these natives were capable of giving their consent or their refusal they should assuredly have been asked to express their wish. But the great mass of them are more ignorant than the Chinese ; and unlike the Chinese or the Siamese they have no national life which binds them together. For hundreds of years they have had only the government of Spain, and consequently have no bond of nationality. Aguinaldo and his army were the representatives of only a small portion of the people. Of the more intelligent Filipinos there was a large party against him and his assumptions. There were millions on the islands who

had never heard of him.   He and his army therefore
could not be taken as expressing the wish of the
natives, or even of a considerable number of them.
Thus Aguinaldo's claim did not rest on the consent of
the governed.

On the other hand, as between the Americans' rule
and that of Aguinaldo, there could be no question
which would more surely and quickly lift the ignorant
natives to a state of civilization where they could intelligently choose their form of government.   Consequently, for the sake of the greatest liberty to the
natives themselves, it seemed our duty to undertake
the government.

In the Philippine Islands, as in Cuba, the question
of citizenship is a remote one.   The immediate question is how best to carry to them the uplifting influences of our national life, the means of intellectual
and moral advancement, the opportunities of liberty,
the security and the penalties of justice.

We maintain our rule over them only as a duty
and for their good.   We are to act at once upon
the lesson which England learned so well at the time
she lost the best of her American colonies, and which
she has since followed so precisely and so advan-
tageously; that is, we are to govern them with even
justice and to protect them with jealous care.   The
sincere purpose to promote their good must not be in
doubt either here or there, or anywhere else in the
world.   It is our duty to help them forward to a self-
government which is constitutional and secure.   If we

can carry them to such a point as that, their government when established is more than likely to be of a
kind like our own, and their people to be worthy of
our fraternity and to desire it.

The action of the United States Government in
ratifying the treaty of peace, and in thus accepting
island empires on both sides of the world, made the
last act in the war with Spain consistent with the first,
and with every intervening act. It proclaimed more
than peace with Spain; it declared for the enlightenment of the millions oppressed by Spain, and for liberty
after enlightenment; it pointed to stability of government and, as soon as may be, for self-government in
the islands; it meant the throwing of our national
protection over peoples who desire to be educated and
to direct their own affairs, and a guaranty that their
desires shall be gratified. In other words, the ratification of the treaty of peace, illumined as it was by the
utterances of the President and by prevailing public
opinion, indicated that the United States accepted
courageously the unforeseen obligations which the war
had thrown upon us.

For the first time in our history we have become re-
sponsible for the self-government of peoples other than
ourselves.

We need apprehend no evil. If our impulses, inspired by our history, lead us to help other peoples,
we may feel sure that they are right; if they impel
us to undertake new enterprises, which are consistent with the character and traditions of our race, we

may well believe ourselves equal to them and go forward.   In no other way shall we show so completely
the value we set upon the great charters of English
liberty, or prove ourselves so worthy of the old Pilgrim
at Plymouth, the ragged Continental soldier at Valley
Forge, the hardy pioneer making new States for us in
the unbroken West, the citizen soldier at Gettysburg,
and the heroic men who gave overwhelming battle for
the liberty of others at Manila and at Santiago.

The war waged by the United States for the rescue
of Cuba was but a part of the world-wide contest for
freedom.   It was by no means an unimportant part.
There was conscience in it which could do nothing but
go forward; there were heroes in it whose acts will add
luster to the pages of human history.   In that it was
waged not for gain nor revenge, not even for the rights
of our own citizens, but for the rights of others and
for the sake of decency in the world, it was upon a distinctly higher plane than any previous national act of
warfare.   In its spirit, its scientific methods, its tremendous force, and its quick accomplishments, it gave
us a new place among the nations of the earth.   Yet
the great event will not accomplish all it should if it does
not give to us a new appreciation of the cost of free
institutions and a new sense of our relations to human
and progress, together with new wisdom, new purposes,
new courage whereby to fill our place completely.

But the spirit of the Republic will not permit even
a partial failure in accomplishing these great ends.

First Steps in the History of Our Country.

By WILLIAM A. MOWRY and ARTHUR MAY MOWRY.

Few books are so fascinating and stirring to boys and girls, either in school or under the evening lamp at home, as " First Steps in the History of Our Country."

The book consists of the personal narratives of 39 of the most distinguished Americans, from Columbus to Edison. Through the stories of these leading personages the history of our country is woven. The personal narratives are told with all the spirit and bright interest of an accomplished story-teller, and abound in anecdote and conversation, and are equally readable both to children and adults.

When a young person finishes this book, he has gained a very fair idea of what AMERICA stands for, and he has also gained a proud idea of what it is to be an American citizen.

It is also a most *fair* book. It gives both sides of disputed questions. Thus, it recognizes what Lord Baltimore did for religious toleration in Maryland as distinctly as it describes what Roger Williams did for religious liberty in Rhode Island. In its portrayal of Calhoun, Clay and Lee, it gives to the South as fair a showing as the North receives in the stories of Webster, Lincoln and Grant.

The book is up-to-date in its recognition of the Spanish war, which is treated in the interesting narrative of the beautiful work done by Clara Barton and the Red Cross Society.

There is not a dull page in it. Though a history, it reads more like a romance. The dullest child who once begins to read this book will not want to lay it down until it is finished.

As a school text-book for elementary grades, or for supplementary reading, or as a book for a child's library, it leads all others.

320 Pages. 213 Illustrations. Retail price, 75 cents.

(For introductory price to Schools, send for Circular.)

"It starts out with the idea that the main thing that the child needs, in order to get his interest aroused in detailed history, is to get first of all a succession of powerful impressions of what the course of American life for the last four centuries means. So it is the significant epochs which are thrown up, and it is a combination of biography and episodes that gives the color and connects the facts. Emerson's saying that every institution is but the lengthened shadow of a man was evidently one of the inspirations of this delightful little book."—*The School Journal.*

Silver, Burdett and Company, Publishers,
Boston.   New York.   Chicago.

Historic Pilgrimages in New England.

By Edwin M. Bacon.

This is the vivid story of early New England, told while standing upon the very spots where the stirring Colonial drama was enacted. The famous places where the Puritans and Pilgrims planted their first homes, the ancient buildings, and the monuments to the wise and dauntless founders of the great Commonwealth are visited, and, while in the atmosphere of the associations, the thrilling narrative of the past is recounted.

The connecting thread is the summer pilgrimage which a thoughtful young fellow from a western college makes to the country of his ancestors. He is accompanied by his father's friend, who talks entertainingly about the memorable facts which the hallowed soil suggests.

The boy's earnest curiosity stands for the interest which some millions of others feel in the same events and personalities and shrines.

Of all the books which describe that country and set forth the significance of the deeds done there,—from the landing of the Pilgrims to the first blow of the Revolution, —this new volume combines, perhaps, the most that is of interest to lovers of Yankee-land. It is accurate. It abounds in facts hitherto unpublished. It gives snatches from early diaries and documents. Disputed stories are sifted until the fabulous elements are cut out.

The style is graphic from start to finish—even statistics are made picturesque.

475 Pages. 131 Illustrations. Uncut edges. Retail price, $1.50. (For introductory price of School Edition send for Circular.)

For School Libraries and Reading Circles, this book appeals to a deep and constant taste. For Supplementary Reading in the higher grades it is a mine of interest and delightful instructiveness.

"'Historic Pilgrimages' abundantly justifies its double purpose of serving both the student's needs of a graphic summary of the history of Massachusetts Bay, and the stranger-visitor's need of a preparation for, and a pleasant keepsake of, his journeyings."—*Boston Journal.*

Silver, Burdett and Company, Publishers,
Boston.   New York.   Chicago.

Songs of The Nation.

Compiled by COL. CHARLES W. JOHNSON.

This is a book which is worthy of its title. No other book published meets so fully and with such fitness, the obvious requirements of a volume of songs which can properly bear the broad title—"Songs of The Nation."

With the new enthusiasm for country and flag, which the sweep of war has intensified, the desire for patriotic songs has deepened. Around the piano at home, in summer hotels, in societies and clubs, in students' rooms, and, most of all, in schools, there is wanted an adequate collection of general songs, broad and exalted in nature and varied enough for many occasions.

Precisely to meet this need is the aim of this volume. It is a superb collection which embodies the patriotic songs most in demand (25 of them), together with many more songs for anniversaries and occasions ; American folk-songs, a group of old religious favorites, the best college songs, etc.

The distinguished compiler, Col. Charles W. Johnson, who for ten years was chief clerk of the United States Senate, has cast the book in conformity to a lofty ideal and with regard to the versatility of public taste.

The introductory chapter on music in public schools, by Mr. Leonard B. Marshall, Superintendent of Musical Instruction of the Boston schools, will be of large practical value to all teachers of music.

The book is of noble appearance, with large type and heavy paper.

4to, 160 pages. Retail price, 75 cents.

(For introductory price to Schools send for special circular.)

"Above all the swarm of small and unsatisfactory collections of patriotic songs 'The Songs of The Nation' stands as the highest in degree, the widest in scope, and the most attractive in appearance. It is a school and college song book no less than a handy book for every home piano."—*The Illustrated American.*

Silver, Burdett and Company, Publishers,

Boston.   New York.   .   Chicago.